Baby's on Fire

baby's on fire

stories

liz prato

Press 53
Winston-Salem

Press 53, LLC
PO Box 30314
Winston-Salem, NC 27130

First Edition

Cover design by Gigi Little
gigilittle.jimdo.com

Author photo by Laura Stanfill

Printed on acid-free paper
ISBN 978-1-941209-15-8

For Michael —
my fire, my water, my earth, my air

acknowledgments

The author wishes to thank the editors of the journals and magazines where these stories first appeared.

"A Space You Can Fall Into," *Carve*, Fall 2013

"The Adventures of a Maya Queen," *Iron Horse Literary Review*, Summer 2008

"Astronomical Objects," *Cream City Review*, Fall 2008

"Covered In Red Dirt," *Hawai`i Review*, forthcoming, Spring 2015

"I See You in the Bright Night," *Storyglossia*, March 2008

"My Son's Father," *Los Angeles Review*, Fall 2009

"Riding to the Shore," *Gold Man Review*, Fall 2014

"When Cody Told Me He Loves Me on a Weird Winter Day," *Hunger Mountain*, January 2011

contents

baby's on fire

Three months after I graduated from Colorado College, and things weren't going well. First, I couldn't find a job. It's not like I was expecting a salaried, corner-office job, either. In this economy, with a liberal arts degree, I knew better. But I couldn't even get my ass hired at Starbucks.

Then my boyfriend cheated on me with a girl he met while volunteering for Habitat for Humanity. I imagined some dreadlocked patchouli-stink chick, but a friend working on the same site told me she wore cut-off shorts and a bikini top and was majoring in Mid-East Studies at Harvard.

Then some asshole destroyed my car while it was parked outside a coffee shop. I was sitting by the window with a latte e-mailing my cousin Jimmy, who'd been backpacking around South America for the last year. A blue SUV swerved across oncoming traffic and plowed into my car. The driver was trashed, and everyone said how lucky it was that no one got hurt.

It got to a point where I couldn't leave my basement apartment. I just laid in bed and watched reality TV marathons. My dad paid for a therapist, who put me on Prozac and suggested I go live with my mom in Portland until I regained solid footing. But ever since my folks split up and Dad moved to Vegas, the ground back home felt like it had seismically shifted, leaving large cracks. It was Spencer, my seventeen-year-old brother, who convinced me. "You're way over-thinking it, Jude," he said. "It's the same fucking house." So I went home, to my mom and my brother.

Two weeks after Spencer convinced me to come back, I stood outside of PDX baggage claim with one giant suitcase. I'd already shipped everything else, my vinyl collection and books and photographs and winter clothes. It meant I'd been living in an empty basement for over a week, which wasn't that great for my mood, but I wanted my things to be home when I arrived. To make it seem more like . . . well, home.

It was hard to tell if the Prozac was working. I wasn't any happier, but I did feel like everything was softly muffled, like being underwater. It was better than feeling hopeless and coffin-still. Besides, the internet assured me, this muted phase would pass.

Spencer's red mohawk leaned out the passenger window of an unfamiliar silver sedan. My mom parked the car and ran over and hugged me like she was afraid I might float away. "Thank god you're home."

"You got a new car?" I asked.

"It's a rental," she said. She was wearing a tie-dyed dress that hung on her like a parachute. "The Volvo's in the shop."

She'd gotten the Volvo in the divorce and Dad got the Honda. He then traded in the Honda for a zippy sports coupe, and soon after drove the zippy sports coupe to his new condo in Vegas.

Spencer picked up my suitcase and hauled it to the trunk.

"How come you guys didn't drive Spike?" I asked. I would have felt welcomed by my brother's old hatchback, spray-painted black with a white skull and crossbones on each door. "Mom didn't think he could make the trip," Spencer said. As if living up to its image, Spencer's car often died on a bridge or a highway or in the middle of an intersection. "Being stranded was all we needed."

I got in the front seat and Spencer sat in back. It was hot, even for Portland in August, and Mom blasted the A/C. Neither of them spoke while we drove. Every once in a while my mom would glance over at me and then into the rearview mirror at Spencer, and then back to the road. She was wearing running shoes with that stupid dress. She never wore her running shoes for anything other than running. They were specifically fitted for her over-pronating foot strike, and she was meticulous about maintaining their integrity.

"What's with your dress?" I asked.

"My dress?" Mom looked down, but not like she forgot what she was wearing. Like she forgot she had clothes on at all.

"Yeah, it's too big for you. And kinda ugly."

"Nice to have you home," Spencer said. "Already a pleasure."

"Well, it is. And why are you wearing your running shoes?" I looked back at Spencer. "I mean, that's weird, right?"

"Mom!" Spencer's voice cracked like he was thirteen. "Say something."

"Honey." Mom reached across the emergency brake and held my hand. "I don't know how to tell you this."

"Tell me what?"

"There was a fire," she said. "It burned down the house. There's nothing left."

"That's bullshit." Cold air burned my lungs like dry ice. There was no way our house really burned down. They would have told me before I moved almost halfway across the country to live in it. "Why would you say that?"

Mom said it happened only two days earlier. She'd been out on a run and Spencer was out with friends. As she ran down the hill, she saw black smoke rising into the air. Then she smelled ash and heard the sirens' howl. She said by the time she sprinted onto our street the scene was just a whir of flashing lights and flames and arcs of water bursting through the air. She stumbled through a line of onlookers and found Spencer in front, with tears streaking his cheeks. They didn't call to tell me about the fire, she said, because I was already miserable and lost enough.

"You would have been freaked out," she said, as we rattled across I-84. "And all alone."

"My stuff," I said. "The stuff I shipped . . ."

"Was in your bedroom."

I stared at the moths smashed on our windshield. The contents of my burned boxes came to me at odd highway intervals. As we passed the Lloyd Mall, I thought of the jewelry box playing "You Are My Sunshine" that Dad gave me on my eighth birthday. Crossing the Willamette River, I saw my college diploma reduced to ash. The Terwilliger exit brought up my melted vinyl collection. *London Calling* was in the wreckage, Paul Simonon's silhouette mangled by heat. Jimmy gave me that album for my sixteenth birthday.

"You should have told me," I choked. "I should've known."

"It's kinda hard to find the perfect way to say 'Hey, by the way, an inferno just destroyed our house,'" Spencer said. "And how's your nervous breakdown going?"

"Why do you have to be such a dick?"

"Me?" Spencer said. "Where's the sympathy for us? We saw the fucking house burn down."

"Two days ago," I said. "I just found out—"

"Oh yeah," he said. "And I'm all adjusted because it's been two whole days."

Mom swerved the car to the side of the road. The tires screeched and all three of us lurched. She turned on the windshield wipers, but said nothing.

She looked so stupid in that gigantic hippy-dippy dress. God, what was she going to wear to work? That dress wasn't good enough for baggage claim, much less a law firm. But that was all she had, this borrowed dress, or her running shorts and shirt. In the trunk I had shorts and tank tops and sundresses and sandals. A hot pink hoodie, and assorted underwear. My mother didn't have underwear and Spencer was forever clad in a T-shirt that said "The Pope Smokes Dope." I could see him graduating from high school, applying for jobs, getting married in that shirt. He'd be buried with the Pontiff smoking a doobie on his chest.

"Come on." I touched my mother's hand. The silence was too cold. "Let's go."

She pulled back onto the highway and I turned on the radio. U2 welcomed me back to Oregon. "The Edge is a poseur," Spencer said.

My mother and I agreed.

The hotel looked like a suburban condominium complex, with a swimming pool and a combination lobby/dining area where complimentary breakfast was served. "It's pretty decent," Spencer said. "You can make your own waffles."

Spencer and I shared a bedroom, which we hadn't done since we were kids. I hauled my suitcase on top of one bed while he opened the window a crack. He reached underneath a pillow and pulled out a baggie of weed and a brass pipe.

"You rescued that?" I asked. He'd bought the pipe while visiting me two Thanksgivings ago in Colorado. We'd boycotted the event back

home—our parents were still pretending like everything was okay—
and ate an orphan's dinner with other students stranded for the holiday.

"I was out scoring weed when the house went boom." Spencer
stuffed a green bud into the bowl and sparked it.

"Have you talked to Dad?"

Spencer blew out smoke and handed me the bowl. "He said I
could come live with him."

"You gonna do it?" I was careful not to light my bangs on fire. I'd
done it once before, when I was seventeen. The smell of burning
hair was not a good one. I couldn't imagine the smell of an entire
house. Cotton and wood and enamel and toxic synthetics, food in
the refrigerator and soup in the pantry. I inhaled the weed deeply,
forcing all those other smells away.

"Are you kidding? It's a hundred and twenty degrees there." After
living in the Northwest his whole life, Spencer probably thought he
would melt. "Hey, Jimmy's having a party tonight. To raise money
for us, get donations, shit like that."

"He's back?" I hadn't heard from Jimmy since before I graduated.
But that's what it was like with us. Intermittent.

"Do you think it's okay to leave Mom?" Spencer asked.

I thought of Jimmy's bed from over a year ago, a narrow single in
his dorm room. I'd visited him the weekend after Mom and Dad
announced their divorce. We drank cheap beer and smoked weak
weed and fell asleep on the mattress with our backs pressed together.
That was the last time we were that close for that long.

"We should go," I said. "I bet Mom could use some time alone."

Jimmy lived in an old two-story kit house, once pretty and practical
with four rooms on the bottom, four rooms on top. Decades of lazy
landlords and twenty-something renters had beaten the house down.
It was like an aging drug addict now, tired and ugly and willing to do
anything for one last fix.

Party-goers crowded the porch, leaning against an old wood
railing. Music I didn't know spilled out open windows. That was
just like Jimmy: he always knew the cool bands. Inside, the house
was hot and heavy with too many people and not enough air. Jimmy
was in the kitchen with a bunch of skinny girls and skinny guys.
Jimmy was the skinniest of them all, or maybe just the longest. There

was an unfamiliar scar on his face, between his jaw and his cheekbone. It was at least an inch long, shaped like a backwards C.

"My homeless cousins!" He smacked Spencer a high-five, then opened his arms to hug me. I had to stand on my toes, and Jimmy had to reach down. Then he grabbed an aluminum pot off the top of the refrigerator. The pot contained dozens of crumpled bills and clanky change. "We've already raised sixty-three dollars for you guys," he said. "And there's a box with ramen and T-shirts and shit on the back porch."

"Do we know any of these people?" I asked. No one looked familiar, but nothing felt familiar, either. Fire shock, I guessed.

"Hey, I made a mix for you guys," Jimmy said. "Hang on." He went into the living room, to the stereo. Seconds later, "Burning Down the House" was blasting through the dense air.

"Nice!" Spencer yelled. "Now where's the keg?"

We trailed Jimmy to the back porch, where he handed us plastic cups. "It's just PBR," he said. "We kinda had to scrimp."

"No problemo," Spencer said. "I've got some A-plus dope." He pulled the baggie and pipe from his cargo shorts and loaded up the bowl.

A girl in a black tank top approached us. She was skinny, like the rest of Jimmy's friends. "You're the guests of honor?"

"So to speak," I said, taking the pipe from Spencer.

The girl had tattoos up and down both arms, golden goddesses in red gowns. "You lost everything?"

"Everything," Spencer said.

"You're lucky," she said. "The chance to give up attachments to material possessions. To start from an empty place. That's a gift from the divine." She pressed her hands together in front of her chest and bowed her head down, then backed away.

I didn't know if it had really happened. If it was the Prozac or the fire shock or the shitty beer and weed kicking in.

"She's been taking classes at the Dharma Center," Jimmy said. "Just spent an entire week breathing."

My mom and Spencer must have breathed in some heavy, black air as they watched the house burn.

Spencer asked, "Hey, is Belinda around?"

I had no idea who Belinda was.

"Said she was coming by," Jimmy said through smoke in the back of his throat.

"I'm gonna take a lap and see if she's here." Spencer walked back into the house, where XTC was singing about fire and love—or maybe lust—and animals in a panic to escape what's impossible to escape.

"Wish he hadn't taken that pipe with him," I said. I needed to suppress everything that was trying to pierce through my haze: Dad, college, boyfriend, car, home, me.

"Come on," Jimmy said. "I hid the good booze in my room."

Jimmy's first-floor room was barely larger than a walk-in closet. I would have believed it was just that, except it had a window that faced the blackness between his house and the neighbor's. Plastic milk crates stacked five high and five long lined one wall, holding Jimmy's jeans and T-shirts and books. On another wall hung a red and black poster of Che Guevara. The other wall was blank.

"Take a seat," he said.

I sat on the futon on the floor. It was wider than the mattress in Jimmy's old dorm. He reached up to the top row of milk crates, which alternated between orange and red. He pulled out a clear bottle and plopped down next to me. I swallowed spicy vodka. It burned the way it was supposed to. Screechy vocals seeped through the walls.

Baby's on fire, and all the laughing boys are bitching.

"Who is this?" I asked.

"Eno," he said. "Early Seventies."

The only Brian Eno I knew was ambient and arrhythmic, forcing me into a meditative stance. Music for airports, the kind airports never really played. But this song pushed against me from the inside, pissed as shit and dying to break out.

I touched the scar on Jimmy's cheek. I traced the top of the C, went into the curve, and fell off the bottom. "How did that happen?"

"Vespa accident in São Paulo." Jimmy took a long, slow drink. "So, are you okay?"

"I don't have a house," I said. "Or a job. Or a life plan. So, no. Not really." I didn't even have a college diploma anymore.

"Everyone our age is just starting out." His knees were bent, rising up high. "We already don't have a lot of stuff, right? We rent rooms, work shitty jobs—"

"You sound like that girl." I stood and looked into the milk crates. I fingered the spines of books by Kerouac, Vonnegut. Nabokov.

"What girl?"

"The Dharma girl."

Jimmy was standing behind me. He was hot, that way. "It's just hard to know what to say." His hands folded over my shoulders, front and back, and twisted me to face him. There was almost a foot between our noses, mine pointing up, his pointing down. "Look at you," he said. "All grown up."

I stood on my toes and Jimmy reached down. I could taste he'd been drinking something before the vodka, before the pot, something other than cheap beer. Something with bright berries that I wanted to stain my tongue, my throat, my gut. We didn't speak until Jimmy was stripped bare, behind me, with my face pressed inside a red milk crate. He started to push his way inside of me, but stopped. "You still need some warming up," he said.

I grabbed Jimmy's hips, pulled him inside me. It was a rough, scathing burn, and he tried to take it easy, but I wouldn't let him. From the next room, Bono screeched about the sun burning black. About the moon running red. About pulling and falling and coming home.

"I can't believe you put this song on," I said into the crate.

Jimmy's voice was nothing but fast breath. "What?"

"U2," I said. "The Edge is such a poseur."

"Jude." Jimmy stopped, deep inside. "What the fuck are you talking about?"

"What?"

He pulled me upright so his chest was against my back. "We're having sex."

"I know."

"Jude . . ." He kissed my shoulder. The upside-down C scratched against my neck.

"I know," I said again.

"Let go," Jimmy said.

I wasn't sure what he was talking about—there was so much to talk about, but I couldn't remember the last time I'd really talked about anything, not even to that therapist, to whom I mostly cried—

but I decided to shut up. For the next few minutes, at least. Until the burn went away.

I found Spencer on the front porch with some henna-haired girl. Belinda. Spencer e-mailed or texted me once a week, and he'd never mentioned her. They were leaning in so close that at first I thought they were sharing a joint or a kiss. It turned out they were just talking, talking so close only the other could hear.

"I'm wiped," I said. "Can you run me home?" I wanted to pull back the word "home," this thing we no longer had, but my mind was too fogged to search for what was right.

Spencer's eyes were dismissive and black. "Wait by Spike," he said. "I'll be there in a sec."

I laid on Spike's hood. I could only make out two stars in the light-polluted sky. In the Rocky Mountains the sky was littered with exploding stars and white dwarfs, with archers and twins and the dust of Earth. Entropy had seemed so beautiful there.

Spencer's boots smacked down the sidewalk, and he slammed Spike's door behind him. As soon as he turned on the ignition, post-industrial punk blared from his stereo. He didn't move to turn it down.

We drove with the windows open, past strip malls and battered neon signs. The smell of fresh-cut grass swarmed through Spike's open windows. I finally saw signs of the familiar. We passed the bakery that handed me free cookies when I was a little kid. The greasy hamburger joint where I worked my first job. The church where I went to pre-school. Dad taught me to ride a bike there, on a steep hill in the parking lot. He let go of the bike and I flew down the hill. I rushed toward the cement embankment at the end of the lot, and didn't know how to stop. So I jumped. I scraped up my knees and my elbows and my face. Nothing was broken, though, so the next day Dad made me get back on.

I turned down the stereo. "Hey, can we—"

Spencer turned it back up.

I flicked off the knob. "What the fuck? I was about to say something."

"So speak," Spencer said. "I'm on the edge of my seat."

"I want to see the house."

Spencer looked out the window. The wind flapped his limp mohawk into a torrent of red strands. "Why?"

"I should," I said. It was too abstract, otherwise. Something made up, like a picture on the internet that had been photoshopped beyond truth. "I need to."

"It's not like you think it is."

I thought it was just an empty hole, like a tornado from *The Wizard of Oz* had lifted our house from the foundation and flung it across the sky. "That's why I need to see it."

"Okay," Spencer said. "But don't say I didn't warn you."

A jagged skeleton remained. Suburban street lamps cast an alien glow on the wreckage. Our blackened chimney rose out of the charred rubble, like something found under Pompeii. Spencer stood by his car while I ducked carefully under yellow tape cordoning off the debris. It seemed like the tape itself could fall and crush me with the slightest misstep. There were splintered clumps and blackened forms that I recognized as couch, lamp, stove. Artifacts from any family, anywhere. Our vacation photos had disintegrated. The upright piano and sheet music incinerated. Personalized coffee mugs crushed.

My bedroom had been on the second floor, over what was once Dad's den. As soon as he moved out, Mom turned his den into a yoga room with sage walls and long mirrors. I wondered if my old bed and bookcase had fallen through the floor, shattering my mother's mirrors. Or maybe they turned to smoke and were lifted to the sky.

"That was some fucked up shit," Spencer said. He was standing on the other side of the yellow tape, arms folded across his chest, a cigarette glowing near his lips.

I spread my legs into a riding stance, feeling like the earth might buckle beneath me. Fire. Tornado. Earthquake. "We're always going to be those people," I said. "The people whose house burned down."

"Not that." Spencer threw down his cigarette and crushed it under the heel of his boot. "You and Jimmy. At his house. That was totally messed up."

My fingers went numb, and then my toes, but my chest and neck burned. How could he know? There was no way anyone could hear us over the music. There was no way to see in . . . except for that one window, facing the black.

I reached for denial, but came up empty. "Spence—"

"He's our cousin." Spencer continued digging his heel into the dirt. "You know it's illegal, like, all over the place."

"Only in America." As if the law was the point. As if it was the arbiter of right and wrong, of what matters and what doesn't. My voice shook while the rest of me stayed statue still. All I wanted was to move. To twitch. To break. "And only in part of it. It's just this puritanical societal construct ¯"

"College has taught you some great theories, really great!" Spencer said. "But maybe you should re-read your fucking Freud. Or maybe—here's a thought—take an ethics class. You and Jimmy, both."

"Maybe I wouldn't be standing here if you hadn't gone out to buy your precious pot," I said. "Maybe you could have stopped the fire. How's that for a theory, Spence?"

He threw his car keys at me. They hit my chest, then fell to the ground. Spencer turned and went into streetlights that made him glow fluorescent yellow, and then dissolve.

I got hopelessly lost trying to navigate Spike back to the hotel. It took me nearly an hour. The air inside our room was barren and cold. The tears and pot and Jimmy made my head feel bloated, my stomach hollow.

Spencer wasn't in the bedroom. My side was littered with dirty clothes thrown in heaps. Spencer's side was immaculate with his new poverty. There was nothing in the room that made it his. None of his band fliers or graphic novels or tattered T-shirts.

I started rooting through my piles. I separated clothes by color, even though I didn't know where we'd do laundry. The door to the suite outside the bedroom closed and I hoped it was Mom, even though I knew it wasn't. Spencer threw open our bedroom door, making it crash against the wall.

"I could've been sleeping, you know," I said.

He stamped across the room, stepping on my piles of laundry. "You don't own this room," he said. "You can't just leave your shit everywhere."

"Fine." I picked up the hot pink hoodie and threw it at him. "I'll pick up." Then I threw a tank top at him, then capri pants, then a sandal. I even threw my plastic bottle of Prozac at him. He batted each item down like a pro goalie. I wadded up a black T-shirt and hurled it at his chest. He smacked it to the ground, but something caught his eye. "This is mine!"

He bent over the forlorn heap. It was Spencer's Sex Pistols shirt, with *God Save the Queen* taped over Queen Elizabeth's mouth and eyes. After the last time he'd visited me in Colorado, I'd found it wadded up in a corner. Black clothes were like that—they sometimes looked more like shadows than shirts. It was too big for me, so I rarely wore it. But still. Just owning it made me feel cooler than I was.

"You've had my shirt this entire time?" he said, standing. "I don't have a fucking change of clothes and you've been hiding this?"

"I haven't been hiding it," I said.

"Yeah, right!"

"Well, why didn't you just go to the mall or the thrift store and get some new clothes?" I asked, hands on my hips. "You're not *required* to be pathetic, you know!"

Spencer slumped down on the edge of the bed. He stared at Queen Elizabeth's wrinkled face. "I don't know," he said. "It just didn't . . ." He looked up at me, limp red strands hanging over his eyes.

"I'm sorry," I said, and I was. And not just because Spencer had been wearing the same shirt since the house burned down, but because it was pathetic of me to think hanging onto his shirt mattered. Spence was Spence and I was me, no matter what clothes clad our bodies.

I crossed the room and touched the black cotton hanging from his hands. "I'll iron it."

"We don't *own* an iron."

"Hotel rooms have irons," I said, which I'd always thought was asinine. Who wanted to do chores while on vacation? People went away to escape the mundane.

I pulled at his shirt. At first, we engaged in an infinitesimal tug-of-war, a push and pull, toward and away. Then Spencer let go. In the suite's living room I set up an ironing board. I stood and waited for the iron to heat while Spencer slept.

I woke ten minutes before breakfast ended. Spencer's bed was made and he was gone. The sky was overcast, and the air was moist. I hauled ass down to the lobby, which smelled like coffee, malt, and fried pork. Spencer sat at a small table staring at sports highlights on TV. An outfielder chased down a shallow fly ball.

"Where's Mom?" I asked.

"She went to work." The Queen Mum stared back from Spencer's chest. He held up a Dixie cup filled with off-white sludge. "Waffle batter. There was only one left, and some preppy bitch almost took it." He watched tennis highlights. Back and forth. Back and forth. Out.

I walked to the waffle bar. I poured the sludge into the iron and clamped it shut. Batter squeezed and sizzled while I poured weak coffee, gathered shriveled bacon. At the small table, Spencer had stacked his plates to make room for me.

"Mom heard from the fire inspector," he said. He wasn't looking at the TV anymore, but at the swimming pool outside. Two little kids splashed in the water—one boy, one girl—not seeming to mind the gray air. Their mom and dad sat nearby in lounge chairs. "It was an overloaded circuit."

The little girl put her hands on her brother's shoulders and pushed him down. He must have grabbed her from beneath, because soon she went under too. The water turned glassy. Serene. I tried to remember how long I could hold my breath underwater when I was little. Spencer and I used to have contests to see who could hold it longer, but he'd always make me laugh.

The pool's surface was shattered by a raindrop. Then another, and another. The kids bobbed to the top and climbed onto the concrete deck. The parents wrapped large towels around small, slippery bodies. Spencer and I watched the family dash inside. The smell of burning waffle batter hung like storm clouds in the air.

when cody told me he loves me on a weird winter day

Cody and I are sitting side-by-side on a picnic table, looking toward the Rocky Mountains covered by ponchos of snow. Black-necked geese are honking, and I'm thinking, *They must be lost. They shouldn't be in Denver. They should be in Acapulco.* The concrete slab is cold under my butt, but the mile-high sun is warm and bright. It makes us both squint. That's when Cody says, "Meg, I think I'm falling in love with you." So I say I think I'm falling in love with him, too.

Two months ago we were just friends swilling Tennessee whiskey to numb respective heartaches. Next thing you know, he's telling me he loves me, and I'm thinking I love him back. For a second or two, that seems just fine. Then Cody says:

"But here's the thing. I'm insanely busy right now. Between teaching and getting ready for this installation in three weeks, I just don't have time to start a new relationship. It wouldn't be fair. So, I think we should put things on hold for a month or so, and then see where we stand."

Where did the lost geese go? They aren't honking anymore. The breeze isn't blowing the bare tree branches. A car hasn't driven by the park in a long time. It's all so quiet that I can't pretend I didn't quite hear him and say *What?*

Cody looks at his watch. "Shit. I've got to get to my studio. I was supposed to meet a student there at four." He jumps off the picnic table and stands in front of me. He blocks out the sun, and I don't have to squint anymore. "Okay." He holds my gloved hand. "I love you."

This time I don't say it back. This time I just say, "Uh-huh," and listen for the wing-beat of geese.

INTERIOR: MY APARTMENT—TWO MONTHS EARLIER

I'm on my couch. CODY is on my floor. His girlfriend just broke up with him; my boyfriend just broke up with me. We're passing a Jack Daniel's bottle back and forth. This makes me look tough.

CODY: So, in case it didn't suck enough, now I also don't have a date for Celia's fundraiser.

ME: They could've at least waited until after the party to break up with us.

CODY: (handing me the bottle) We could go together.

ME: I can think of worse.

The geese are back. "Where the fuck were you when I needed you?" I say. They honk, honk, honk. Some nonsense from the *Tao Te Ching.* The sun is falling south. It will be cold and dark soon. Across the street from the park is a coffee shop, the kind with dreadlocked girls and scratched wood tables and frou-frou drinks with the comfort of vanilla and spice. It's warm inside, with steam shooting from the espresso machine, and music shooting from the stereo. I order a molto grande latte with cinnamon and nutmeg. It's okay for me to have that much caffeine, now that I'm not pregnant anymore.

Celia and Cody were a couple after college, in another decade, another century. Cody lives in a world where he's still friends with his ex-girlfriend from another century, so he's friends with her husband—my brother, Nate—too. I was a bridesmaid at their wedding and Cody a groomsman, so you'd think we'd have hooked up taffeta-drunk then. It's the only acceptable scenario for bedding your sister-in-law's ex. But I was blindly devoted to a long distance boyfriend, and Cody brought some pretty girl. That's the way it had been ever since.

Celia's the Executive Director of Act Out!, a nonprofit that goes into schools and teaches kids to express their feelings through improv. Sometimes I help Celia come up with scenarios to get the kids started.

Things like: YOU and TWO FRIENDS are hanging out together, when one pulls out a bong. Or: YOU and A GUY are getting hot and heavy, but don't have a condom. Sometimes I come up with these scenarios even when Celia doesn't need them.

Before Christmas, Act Out! hosted a black-tie fundraiser. It was attended by Denver's society set, and by Celia and Nate and Cody and me. Nate rented a limo so we could all get insanely drunk on French champagne without risking anybody's life. It's the sort of extravaganza that a grad school dropout working in a bookstore would never get to attend, but Celia and Nate made it possible. The party was in a mansion that no one has lived in for a hundred years but gets rented out for weddings and high-class affairs. I could see why Celia wanted to stage the party there instead of a generic ballroom at the Marriott. The mansion had a real Louis XIV feel to it. And maybe that's how we got in trouble. We thought we were untouchable.

INTERIOR: OPULENT ROOM IN MANSION—SEVEN WEEKS EARLIER
Velvet couches and chairs, a gilded portrait of some old woman. TWO MEN, TWO WOMEN, dressed to the nines. They're drinking and laughing like the cast of a sitcom. CELIA asks if anyone's ever had a ménage-a-trois. This is not a sitcom.

CODY: (slurping from crystal flute) Been there, done that, the T-shirt was too small.

ME: (laughing) There were T-shirts at yours? There was an utter lack of them at mine!

CODY: (jade eyes fogged by champagne) What do you say, Meggie? You, me, and who else? You want another man or another woman to complete the triangle?

ME: Do you mean your masculinity could stand up to another man?

NATE: (my brother) Disturbing mental picture here, kids.

CODY: Honey, I don't know if my masculinity could stand up to *you.*

We were all quite sophisticated and witty.

It's not like Cody and I had never been flirty before, flirty in that way you get when you've known someone a long time but he's your sister-in-law's ex-boyfriend, so he's off-limits. Flirty in that way you get when you've had a little too much—but not *too* too much—to drink and you're both dumbly devoted to others, so you know it's harmless and will go nowhere. We'd flirted like that before. But we'd never flirted before with broken hearts, with Cody in a tuxedo after watching Cary Grant movies to figure out how to act suave and debonair, and me in a Little Black Dress—not looking as much like Holly Golightly as I secretly want, but still pretty good for a redhead with hips—with much-too-much champagne and the two of us alone in the back of the limo with the streetlights throwing neon across our faces. All that took us upstairs to my apartment. There was no "what does this mean" discussion. There was no stating of the obvious—*I don't want to ruin our friendship.* There was Cody's long, lanky body, a little soft in the belly, but hard in the right places, in my right places. There was my couch, and a rocking chair, and lastly, my bed, and when you end up in that many places that many times, sooner or later your birth control situation is bound to get "dubious." That's what Cody called it six weeks later, when I told him I was pregnant.

"And you're sure?" he asked.

"I took two tests," I said. The first one had been at home. First Response, it was called, as if the EMTs were going to arrive and give me CPR. I lay on the bathroom floor listening for their sirens for a long time. My faucet *drip drip dripped*, and the pipes banged above my head. No first responders ever arrived to pick me off the floor, so I got up and drove to the health clinic.

Since Cody lives in a world where he's friends with his ex-girlfriend and her husband, he also acted like a Stand Up Guy when he discovered some woman who wasn't his girlfriend was pregnant. "I'm going to support you no matter what you do, okay?" he said. "If you get an abortion, I'll be there and help pay for it. If you have the baby, same thing." That's how it is with Stand Up Guys: they don't tell you what to do.

I'd always figured, "Oh, if I have an unwanted pregnancy, I'll just get an abortion." In my head I actually said "unwanted pregnancy," probably because I majored in Women's Studies, and even though they say the personal is political, what they really mean is it's all academic. The GRE question would go something like this:

If the subject is 31 years old and makes $12 per hour while working 30 hours a week in a bookstore with 1.5 degrees and 3.5 ex-serious boyfriends (none of whom are the father) and she still wears Doc Martens and never carries tissues in her purse, will she: a) make a crappy mother; b) get an abortion; c) feel soul-crushing regret no matter what she decides?

I invited Celia and Nate out to lunch to break the news. They both came from work dressed in suits while my thrift store sweater pilled. After our drinks arrived, I said, "I slept with Cody."

"Like, sexually, you mean?" Celia said.

"No," I said. "I'm making a production of us napping together."

Nate sipped iced tea through a straw. "You and Cody? Seriously?"

"Seriously."

"Well, that's . . . that's kind of . . ." Celia started laughing. And she kept laughing. So did Nate. In fact, they were whooping it up so big that they didn't notice I wasn't even cracking a smile. "God, that's funny!"

"It is?"

"It is." Celia grabbed Nate's forearm. "I don't know why."

"Because it's Cody!" Nate said, and they laughed some more.

"Okay," I said. "Well, if you thought Act One was funny, wait until you hear Act Two." I thought I could hitch a ride on their laughter, but before any words came out of my mouth, tears came out of my eyes. I told Nate and Celia about the two tests. Celia held my hand and Nate gave me big brother eyes, like I'd just lost my ice cream cone to the summer sidewalk.

"What are you going to do?" he asked.

"I don't know," I said.

Nate pulled a red Moleskine notepad from his breast pocket and plunked it on the table. He took out a pen and made a list of the reasons I shouldn't keep the baby. It's the same notebook where he jots down ideas about how to re-design the interiors people pay him to re-design. Sometimes it's about changing the wall color to "Butter Up" or "Tiger Eye." Sometimes he moves an entire staircase. His list for me said:

— 31
— single

— tiny apartment
— Cody
Celia picked up the notepad. "Sweetie, this isn't exactly supportive."

"I'm being pragmatic," Nate said. "I don't think she can get a Pell Grant for this."

"Well, maybe this isn't an entirely pragmatic decision," Celia said. "Maybe it should be a little emotional."

"My sister is knocked up with the love child of your ex-boyfriend," Nate said. "This is the best I can muster."

Nate and Celia's reasons for not having kids included: expensive, noisy, stressful, messy, time-consuming. Celia admitted that anyone who stopped for one rational moment to consider the consequences of having kids wouldn't do it, but people do it anyway, all the time. Biological drive usually trumps reason. But Celia figured she and Nate must be ruled by something else, some intangible intelligence which overrode their biological drive. When I tried to plug into my intangible intelligence, all I got back were pipes banging above my head. I was curled on the floor, wishing the EMTs would arrive.

I took the pen from Nate's hand. I made my own list. It said:
— it's not like I'm 16
— no other prospects on the horizon
— would it be so bad, really?
— Cody

Cody's studio is in the basement of an old church that's no longer a church. Every time I step foot in it, I'm still surprised that a church can be anything other than a church. But I guess it's still got to be something after all its believers go away. I walked into the studio without knocking, not that Cody could have heard my knocking if I did. He was welding a frame together. Not a picture frame, but a doorframe, as if he were building a house within a house. I stepped around the other side of the frame and waved my hands at him. He turned off the blowtorch.

"Is there any real reason I couldn't have this baby?" I asked.

He hadn't taken off his welding goggles. "No, not really."

"Between the two of us and our friends and family, there'd be enough people to help us take care of it, right?"

"Probably." He was still grasping the blowtorch.

I took a deep breath. "I want to keep the baby, Cody. Is that okay?"

"I told you I'd support you no matter what," Cody said.

It sounded like a good answer, like the right answer, like the sort of answer that allowed us to move forward. But, I guess if I were really paying attention I might have wondered why he never took off his goggles. Why he kept grasping a blowtorch in the basement of a church where no one worshipped anymore.

INTERIOR: NATE AND CELIA'S DINING ROOM—TEN DAYS AGO

ME, CODY, NATE, AND CELIA. An adult dinner party. It's important to have adult dinner parties, instead of hanging out at coffee shops like the cast of a sitcom. CODY arrives late, slow, muted. In the middle of dinner, he gets up for the bathroom. His legs come out from under him and he hits the floor. The dinner party turns to: panic.

EVERYONE: (shouting) Cody, are you okay?

CELIA: (slapping Cody's cheek) Cody, wake up!

ME: (with unfamiliar shrillness) He only had two glasses of wine! That's all!

NATE: Well, there may be one other thing.

(Celia and I look at him)

NATE: He borrowed some Valium from me yesterday. He said he's been having panic attacks.

ME: How many pills?

NATE: Just two. That's it.

CODY: (mumbling) Why am I on the floor?

CELIA: (standing) He's just fucked up, that's all.

ME (voice-over) *Ladies and gentlemen: the father of my child.*

When Cody opened his scratched wood door the morning after our adult dinner party, he looked like how a five-year-old would draw a hangover—if five-year-olds drew hangovers: gray and fuzzy with bloodshot eyes.

"How are you feeling?" I asked.

"Mostly embarrassed."

We sat on his couch, which was a futon folded up to look like a couch. At night he folded his futon down to look like a bed. Cody stared right at me for a good minute, as if I might not realize he was about to say something serious otherwise. "I still live like I'm in college," he said. "I have no savings, and anytime I do have extra money, I spend it backpacking around Peru."

There were sirens outside. Not the kind that lure men to the rocks. The kind that grow and fade, get sharper and louder, then dull and sad. Other sounds probably do that, too, maybe even girls on rocks, but in Physics 101 I learned about sirens on police cars and ambulances and fire trucks.

"Meg, you're probably a lot better off not having a baby with me."

"Oh my God." I felt how a five-year-old would draw amazement: wide eyes, open mouth, eyebrows high. "You don't even hear yourself, do you?"

"What do you mean?"

"I mean you're so freaked out that you had to drink yourself—" I pointed at him three or four times in a row, "—and drug yourself into a stupor last night, but you're sitting there acting like this is all some . . . you know . . . *favor* you're doing me."

"I'm just kind of realizing that this isn't exactly how I pictured my life going," Cody said.

"Well, it wasn't part of my master plan either."

Say it. *Say it, say it, say it, say it.* The sirens outside wailed say it, say it, say it.

Then he said it. "I'm not sure I want to be a father."

We said a lot of things, then. The word *responsibility* got bandied about. That word doesn't stick, though. Not for very long. No sooner would it land on Cody than he'd throw it back. Then it would land on me, and I'd bat it away. Soon, the word got tired, and it fell into a heap on the floor.

"You know, it's not like I don't already feel like a total asshole about this," Cody said.

"Am I supposed to feel bad that you feel bad?" I asked.

"Oh, for Christsake, Meg!" Cody sprang up from the futon-folded-into-a-couch. "Will you give me a fucking break!"

And there it was: We had turned into a bitter, disillusioned couple—without ever being a couple.

"Forget it, Cody," I said. "I'll take care of it. You know, every time I told someone you were the father, they laughed, and now I know why." I heard how mean it was, but I couldn't afford to take it back. "Pretending that things are different—that you're different—simply because you want to be or because I want you to be won't make it true. So this is me giving you the break you want. You're off the hook." I turned from him and headed for the door.

"That's not what I want!" he said.

"Don't." I pointed back at him. "Don't lie. It'll just make us both hate you more."

And then I did the drama thing: I slammed the door. I ran down the stairs of his building, and I slammed the door again. It hardly made a sound.

My car was cold, the glass fogged. I drove home with windows down. The sky was purple. Nate would call it aubergine. To Cody, it's probably violet. It all means the same when painted on a winter sky: snow was on the way.

I called my brother from my apartment. "Cody's bailing on me."

"That fucking prick. Celia!" Nate yelled behind him, beside him, to another room. "That fucking prick is bailing on Meg!"

"I can't raise a baby on my own," I said, blowing my nose into Nate's ear.

"Sweetie . . ." Nate's voice faded off, as if it was looking for something. Or maybe it was just retrieving what was already there. "If you need help, Aunt Celia and Uncle Nate would love nothing more."

"But you don't want kids."

"This isn't the same," he said.

Nate would be a great uncle, or a father, or some sort of male role model. He would paint the nursery Mango Orange and sit in a jacquard chair with the baby against his chest.

He whistled. "The storm's really picking up."

The sky outside my windows was littered with snow, like a tickertape parade for heroes returning home. "I know."

INTERIOR: MY APARTMENT—LATER THAT NIGHT

I'm lying in bed, trying to read and trying to drink herbal tea. I hate herbal tea. Stuck to the ceiling above are fluorescent planets and stars left by a previous tenant. My hand is on my belly. My eyes are on my hand.

ME (speaking softly): Is there anyone in there?
MY BELLY: (no answer)
ME: Tell me what you want.
MY BELLY: I want some cookies.
ME: Who is that?
MY BELLY: You know.
ME: No. I don't.

There was a knock on my door near ten o'clock. There was no one who could be knocking on my door near ten o'clock, not in that storm, not when cars couldn't pass through the snow.

Cody stood there holding snowshoes in his hands, big unwieldy looking things that could also be squash racquets. Not that I'd ever met anyone who played squash, but if I had, their racquets would look like Cody's snowshoes. Or maybe they were more like animal traps.

"I feel crappy about the way we left things," he said.

I thought of telling him to go home. And he'd say, But it took me so long to get here in the snow, and then I'd say, Well, who asked you to come here in the snow, anyway? and then we'd bicker until I felt like I'd punished him enough, but it seemed like the sort of thing that only people in romantic comedies do. I realized that while I was thinking about what I should and shouldn't do, Cody was standing in the hallway waiting for me to invite him in or tell him to go, and his having to wait was good enough for me.

"I guess you should come in," I said.

He took off his coat and shook out his hat, scattering tickertape all over my floor. We sat on my couch, which is always just a couch, except for that night when Cody and I made it into something more.

"I can't help that I'm scared shitless," he said. "But it doesn't mean I'm backing out on you."

"I don't want you to be there only because you want to be a Stand Up Guy," I said. "I want you to be there because you want to, and you clearly don't."

"No, that's not what I'm saying. I'm just . . . ." Cody closed his eyes and shook his head and looked at the floor. Then he turned his head and opened his eyes, and then he looked at me. "Aren't you scared?"

I'd never stopped listening for sirens, not since the first moment I crawled down onto my bathroom floor. And, really, plenty of first responders had shown up since: Nate and Celia and even Cody. The problem was, they could only respond to the acute. I was in it for the long-term.

"Terrified," I said.

"We won't stop being scared once we're actually parents." It was the first time anyone said that word. They'd said mother a lot, and father and baby a lot, and even abortion, but never that word. Me and Cody. Together.

"Let's just do the best we can," he said. "And give each other a break."

Cody put his hand over my stomach. It wasn't much, my stomach, not much more than it was a couple of months ago. "Look what we did, Meggie."

I put my hand over his. "I know."

There was no couch and no rocking chair, no tuxedo or limo or French champagne, and certainly no dubious birth control. It was just soft and quiet and slow. We fell asleep tangled, with the tickertape of heroes forming a blanket on the ground.

The morning was bright: blue sky, yellow sun, white snow. But there was something else, something warm and sticky between my legs. It wasn't until I pulled back the covers that I recognized it as blood.

"Cody!"

He rolled over and mumbled, "What?"

"Cody!" I pointed to the red.

"Oh, shit!" He jumped out of bed. He said *Oh, shit* a few more times and turned circles like a dog getting ready to lie down. Then he pulled on his jeans and a T-shirt, and went to the bathroom. He came back with a warm wash cloth. He cleaned the blood off my thighs, swift and smooth and not weird like it should have been. He handed me sweatpants and a sweater. "I'll go start the car," he said, and took my keys downstairs.

I put on the sweatpants and sweater and socks and shoes. Then I got on my knees at the side of my bed. I looked at the sticky red spot. It wasn't thick and it wasn't thin. I didn't know what it was.

"Hello?" I whispered. "Is anyone in there?"

Cody came back upstairs with my keys in his hand. "Your car won't start."

This is not a story where Cody put on his snowshoes and carried me to the hospital, leaving a trail of bright blood on top of pure white snow. He went next door and borrowed my neighbor's SUV. Cody kept his eyes on the road, his hands at ten and two. No radio.

INTERIOR: A HOSPITAL ROOM—ONE WEEK AGO

ME on an exam table. CODY holding my hand. Some female DOCTOR and an ULTRASOUND TECH huddled between my legs. This is not the ultrasound on TV, against a woman's full stomach with cold gooey gel. This one is inside of me, probing. Is anyone in there?

SOME DOCTOR: Meg, I'm afraid the fetus isn't viable.

ME: I don't know what that means.

SOME DOCTOR: It's means we'll have to perform a D&C.

CODY'S EYES: *Everything will be okay.*

MY EYES: *Are you sure?*

CODY'S EYES: (very clear) *I promise.*

It's been a week since the scene in the hospital. Now there's hardly any snow on the ground, just on the north lawns of buildings and in the shade of giant pine trees. Cody called every day since that day in the hospital, but I was never home. I was shelving books or napping at Nate and Celia's or imagining scenarios for Act Out! by myself. Each time Cody called, he talked to my voicemail. "I just want you to know I'm thinking about you. Maybe we can see each other this weekend. Take a walk and talk." He probably didn't mean to rhyme. So, we went for a walk and we talked, and . . .

We were sitting on the concrete slab, looking at the mountains covered in ponchos of snow. We'd been talking about normal things, about books and his upcoming show and how I was doing, which was fine. Then Cody said, "Meg, I think I'm falling in love with you."

Everything stopped.

The breeze stopped blowing and the trees stopped rustling and the geese stopped honking and the pain and the loss and confusion and fear—it all sat on pause. For the last two months I'd been wandering through an overly scripted scene that I didn't even write.

But on this sunny winter day I knew one thing for sure: that when Cody said he was falling in love with me, he wasn't being the man who he thought he should be or the man he wished he wasn't. He was just being true. Maybe I could just toss away the script, maybe I could be true, too.

I looked at him squinting into the afternoon sun. I squeezed his hand tightly. "I think I'm in love with you, too."

It was such a stupid thing to say. Or, at least, saying it made me feel stupid. Not right away, because right away I felt like I wanted to ride in a hot air balloon and eat fresh strawberries and hike to Machu Picchu and recite Shakespeare and sit in a bubble bath and do the Macarena and have a hundred babies with Cody. He brought my hand to his mouth and kissed the place where our thumbs folded over each other. His lips were cold and chapped. Then he said he didn't have time for a relationship. He didn't have time for me.

The molto grande latte I drank earlier keeps my legs tossing and my torso turning long after I've shut off the light. Above me the haphazard solar system glows fluorescent green. Somewhere beneath me is the blood. It settled there while I was in the hospital, burrowing through my sheets and into the mattress until there was nowhere left for it to go. Sheets can be washed three times and then thrown away. But mattresses, they just get sponge-cleaned and flipped by Celia and Nate.

Cody calls sometime after midnight. "Did I wake you?"

"It's after midnight," I say.

"I was an idiot earlier."

"I know."

"I don't want to wait a month," he says. "I'm just afraid I'll fuck things up."

"You might fuck things up," I say.

"All that stuff about me being insanely busy, that's all true. I mean, that's why I'm calling you at midnight—"

"After midnight."

"Because I just got free. Can you put up with all that for a few more weeks?"

"I've put up with worse," I say, which is true.

"Then let's have noodles," he says. "Tomorrow night. Can you meet me at my studio around nine? I'll order Thai."

"Sure," I say. "Noodles at nine."

I hang up the phone. Noodles at a church where people no longer worship, but maybe they still say prayers. I put my hand over my stomach. It's not much, my stomach, nothing more than it was two months ago. My hand is warm, or maybe it's my belly, or maybe they create heat together. I fall asleep slowly, while sirens sing on the street below.

a space you can fall into

Shelby and her little cousin Janie are sitting on the front porch in Big Springs, Nebraska, only a four-hour drive from Denver, but to Shelby it feels as far as Baghdad. It's so flat in front of her and to every side that she can just see and see until there's nothing left to see. She can't imagine how people get surprised by tornados out here. You could see a goddamn bee coming from a mile away.

"Hey, Shelby, I can fly," says Janie, who's eight, half as old as Shelby. "I take off from the top of the tree." The old cottonwood tree is as tall as the dirty white farm house, and then some.

"That thing's, like, twenty feet tall," Shelby says. She looks at her bright pink phone again to see if her friend Lollie's texted her. Her phone's only got one bar that fades in and out, and that's just too thin a tether to her life.

"It's *fifty* feet," Janie says. "And I climb out my window and then get on the branches and then climb up some more."

"Yeah, right." Shelby texts Lollie: *What r u up 2?* and hopes Lollie's not up to anything too fun.

Shelby's parents sent her to stay on the farm with her aunt and uncle and two cousins while her dad moves out of the house. When Shelby gets back there will just be dusty spaces where her dad's belongings used to be, and nothing where he used to be, just a bad burn in Shelby's belly. A burn she hasn't been able to get rid of since her parents gave her the "we still love you but don't love each other" speech. Shelby knew it was bullshit. She knew her mom still loved her dad. It was her dad who didn't love them anymore.

"I can fly!" Janie says. She's standing on top of a wooden porch chair that looks rickety enough to be splintered by a breeze. "I can fly whenever I feel like it."

"Jesus, get down," Shelby says.

"Admit it!" Janie yells. "Admit that I can fly!"

Shelby knows the danger of believing in what's not real, but she's worried that Janie's going to break an arm on that old chair. "Fine," she says. "You can fly. You're a regular stealth bomber."

"What's that?" Janie asks.

In front of them is the hen house, and beyond that is the pig sty, and every minute Shelby hopes the wind doesn't change too fast. Back behind the house is Shelby's aunt's garden, where she grows tomatoes and lettuce and cucumbers, and from those cucumbers she makes her own pickles. Shelby and her dad put those pickles on nearly everything they ate together—hamburgers, sandwiches, hot dogs and even pizza. He said the best meal he ever had was a sandwich Shelby made for him out of Havarti cheese, red onions, brown mustard and a heaping of farm-made pickles.

Shelby walks away from Janie, toward her aunt's garden, where it always smells like fresh dill.

It's Saturday night and Shelby's boy cousin is going into town and asks if she wants to go, too. He's just graduated from high school but won't be going off to college, not even community college, because Shelby's uncle needs his hands on the farm. Shelby puts on a short black skirt and a red tank top with glitter and silver hoop earrings so that when these small town kids see her they'll know she's from the city.

"You're awfully dressed up for town," her uncle says. He's sitting at the big farmhouse table playing gin-rummy with Shelby's aunt.

"She looks nice," her aunt says, discarding a two of spades. "Shelby, you look nice. Y'all have fun."

"Don't stay out too late," her uncle says. "We got church tomorrow."

The last time Shelby went to church was her grandma's funeral when she was nine. It was in a Catholic church in Denver with a giant white steeple that curved down like a massive water slide. The Ski Slope church, everyone called it. Shelby wondered if her grandma's spirit was going to lift out of her coffin, up to the roof of the church, and then her grandma would slide down the steeple on her butt. Go flying off the end with the wind floating through her skirt.

Shelby's cousin doesn't drive them into town. He starts that way, but instead of making a left turn, he goes right. "Nothing to do in town," he says. "We're going to Ogallala."

It doesn't seem like there could be much more to do in Ogallala than in Big Springs, but it's got a movie theater and some restaurants and a frozen yogurt joint. In the McDonald's parking lot are a load of pick-ups with teenagers hanging out in the truck beds. The radios are playing country and rap and classic rock, making a big mess of noise.

Shelby's cousin goes inside to get some food, but she stays in the truck because she's finally got three solid bars on her cell phone. She calls Lollie, instead of texting her. She can't remember the last time they actually talked on the phone, and Lollie probably can't either, because the first thing she says is, "Oh my God, why are you calling me?"

"It's hip to be retro," Shelby says.

Lollie laughs. "Have you fallen in love with a farmer yet? I want to come to your barn wedding. The pigs and cows can be groomsmen."

"God, these people are so boring I'm gonna kill myself," Shelby says. Just talking on a cell phone makes her think of the time she couldn't sleep and came down to the kitchen for some cereal, and overheard her dad whispering into his cell phone. Her mom was upstairs in bed. "I bet you're having a blast."

"We all got sooo drunk the other night!" Lollie says. "My sister got us a bunch of beer and we went to Cherry Creek dam and I hooked up with Jason Ridgeway."

Jason Ridgeway is an alto sax player in the school jazz band. One day last year he showed up for school and suddenly looked taller and stronger, with a deeper voice. It's like the boys all turned into men overnight.

"Like, *how* hooked up?" Shelby asks.

"Not *totally*," Lollie says. "But we're going out tomorrow, and I'm pretty sure we'll do it then."

Shelby can't believe Lollie's going to lose her virginity before her. Lollie's okay-looking, with straight dirty blond hair and thick bangs, but she doesn't put much effort into how she looks. Lollie's more into being goofy and laughing than cute clothes or make-up or acting cool.

"I don't know," Shelby says. "Jason's not that hot."

"You said he was just a couple of months ago," Lollie said. "He was wearing that baby blue shirt and you said he was cute."

"I said his shirt was cute. Are you going to do it with his shirt?"

"What's wrong with you?" Lollie says. "I thought you'd be happy for me."

"What do I care?" Shelby says. "It's not my virginity."

The girls sit in silence, probably one of the reasons no one calls anymore. With texts, if there's a silence between messages they just figure someone's mother walked in or they had to go eat dinner or even got another text. But it's clear none of this is happening in the space between Shelby and Lollie.

"I've got to go," Shelby says. "My cousin's sitting right here."

They hang up and Shelby gets out of the truck. She can see her cousin standing in line inside McDonald's, laughing with some other kids. Near the back of the parking lot is a guy sitting on the gate of his truck, drinking from a paper bag. He's the only one who doesn't already have some girls with him, around him, near him. Shelby walks over fast at first, and then slow, and says, "Hey."

He looks a little older than Shelby, with some two-day stubble on his hollow cheeks and chin.

"Hey," he says. "Who are you?"

"Shelby," she says. "Can I have some of that?" She nods her chin to the brown paper bag, not knowing for sure what's inside, but figuring it'll be good for the burn inside of her.

He hands her the bottle. "Whiskey," he says. "Think you can handle it?"

"I can handle anything," Shelby says. She's never drank whiskey before, just beer and vodka, and is surprised that something can taste so sweet and so hot at the same time.

"There you are," her cousin says. He hands her a chocolate milkshake. "Hey, Cord. You met my cousin Shelby, I guess?"

"Sure." Cord takes a swig off the whiskey and asks Shelby, "More?"

She takes the top off her milkshake and holds it toward him. "Put it in here," she says, hoping the ice cream will take away some of the burn.

"Too full," he says.

She sticks the straw back in the cup and sucks slowly. She looks up and watches Cord watch her the way the girls in her dad's magazines do when giving head. Cord barely grins. "That's good enough," he says. He pours whiskey into the chocolate shake and Shelby stirs it in.

"Hey, let's go up to the lake," Shelby's cousin says. He calls across the parking lot to a bunch of girls that Shelby sees as nothing but denim. Pants, jackets, probably tank tops, too. "Meet us up at the lake, okay?"

"Yeah, okay!" yells back some girl, and they all pile into a red pick-up.

Cord nods toward his cab. "You wanna ride up front?"

Shelby doesn't answer him, mostly because the ice cream whiskey is still burning her throat and she's afraid if she tries to talk nothing will come out. She just strides up front in her black miniskirt and hops on in.

Cord and Shelby don't talk much on the ride to the lake. It's a short drive, and Cord's got the stereo playing old-fashioned country & western. "I didn't think anyone still listened to this stuff," Shelby says.

"This is real music," Cord says. "Not that Garth Brooks/Keith Urban shit."

The guitar is super twangy and sounds almost Hawaiian, but the man's voice is all country. He's singing about his woman's cheatin' heart. How she cheated on him and even if she doesn't tell anyone, her heart will tell on her by making her cry. Shelby bets it doesn't really work that way. She bets her dad hasn't shed one tear over what he did to her and her mom. When Shelby's mom found out about the other woman he was seeing, she yelled and cried and slammed the refrigerator door so hard that it bounced back open. Shelby didn't even know that was possible, because of the suction strips along the sides, but all the bottles of mustard and pickles and beer smashed to the floor. Her mom ran upstairs to the bathroom and locked the door. Shelby's dad didn't say one word to either of them. He just swept up the shards and threw them in the trash.

It's dark up at the lake and the water looks more black than anything else. Shelby just about believes there's nothing butting up against the banks, just a space you can fall into and never climb out of. She and Cord sit in the back of the truck and wait for the others, who seem to be taking a long time. It's gotten cold, and Shelby didn't bring a sweater. Cord sees her shiver, grabs a blanket from the back of his cab, puts it around her shoulders. She expects it to smell like hay or dust, but it's spicy. Like Cord.

He lights a joint, and since Shelby's smoked weed before she doesn't have to put on an act. Besides, everything's fuzzy from the whiskey milkshake and she's pretty sure she can do just about anything and not feel scared or nervous.

"How old are you?" she asks.

"Twenty." He draws on the joint. "How about you?"

"How old do you think I am?" Lollie's sister told them it's always better to ask this before answering, especially when you meet an older guy. You've got to know whether or not to lie.

"Old enough," Cord says.

When he kisses Shelby she's surprised by how big his tongue seems. It fills her whole mouth, and it tastes sweet and it tastes sour. He pushes her back against the bed of the truck. He doesn't bother to take her skirt off, or her panties, just reaches under and sticks a finger inside her.

"The others will be here soon," Shelby says, even though she suspects the others aren't coming. Not here, not to this place, anyway.

"Do you want me to fuck you?" he says. No one's ever said that word to Shelby before, not like that, not as something she might let him do inside her. She had never wanted it before. She had wanted someone to make love to her, or even just have sex with her. But on the cold, hard bed of a truck and her dad getting farther away, what Cord says feels right. Or, at least like it fits.

Cord takes her panties off but leaves her miniskirt on, and while he fucks Shelby she looks up at the sky and notices it for the first time: you can see stars here. All of them. Every star that was ever made, whether it still exists or not, looks down at Shelby in the back of the brown pick-up truck, and they don't twinkle or glow or any of those other things you expect stars to do. They just burn.

After they're done, Shelby puts her panties back on and gets in the front of Cord's truck. They drive a few minutes around the lake in silence and find her cousin and the denim girls in the red pick-up. Her cousin smiles and asks, "You having fun with all us bumpkins, city girl?"

Shelby mumbles something like "Whatever," then sits on the bank of the lake. Cord sits way over on the gate of his pick-up watching all the others, not drinking or smoking or talking, just smirking with his arms folded. Shelby wishes the lake really were just a black hole, a nothingness that would suck her in and never let her back out again. Maybe then her dad would understand how thrown away he's made her feel.

Shelby's aunt and uncle and little Janie are asleep when she and her cousin get back from Ogallala. She's sharing Janie's room and has to sleep in the bottom bunk bed. Janie's room is pink, but the night dark makes it gray. There's light peeking in from the moon, bending around the branches of the cottonwood tree outside the open window. Shadows of the branches sneak inside, climb around the gray walls. Janie's out cold, and why shouldn't she be? She doesn't know a single thing about cheating hearts or pickle bottles smashing to the floor or getting fucked under searing stars.

There's a big branch right outside Janie's window, like an arm stretched beneath the sill. Shelby climbs through the window, reaching out to the branch above for some balance. She inches towards the trunk of the tree. The branches above are stacked like a Tinkertoy maze, and it's up to Shelby to figure out the right path up, the right path out. She pulls herself up a level and then another and it burns her arms, which matches how she feels where Cord was. The burning in Shelby's arms takes away from the other burn. Makes it less scathing. But it doesn't take long until her arms give out. When she was a kid Shelby could do chin ups on the jungle gym and never get tired. Her mom says that's what happens when girls go through puberty. They lose their upper-body strength.

There's still plenty of tree above Shelby, and she's surprised at how much tree is below her, too. The ground is far enough down that it's hard to believe the tree's a part of it. That she's a part of it. She inches out onto the branch. They're thinner up high than they were down by the window. Maybe trees lose their upper body strength as they grow, too. Shelby peeks out from under the leaves, up at the sky. Those stars are still there, looking down at her, saying, Come on. What are you waiting for?

A breeze makes the leaves shiver. The smell of dill from her aunt's garden whispers by, tingling Shelby's nose. She wishes Janie was awake. Janie could show Shelby how she does it. How she spreads her arms. If she puts them out in front or to her sides. Whether she jumps or flaps or soars. Or maybe she just steps off the branch, and lets the wind take her.

the adventures of
a maya queen

Here I am, perched one-hundred-and-five feet in the sky with the green canopy of the jungle far below. It billows like a giant parachute covering my kingdom. Lording high above it all, I am a Maya Queen.

Peter's blond head rises above that last step of the temple. The steps carved into the sides of the pyramids are tall and steep, which is curious since the Maya were so short. My boyfriend's tall, and he still huffs and puffs and pants. "My quads are killing me," he says. "Why didn't you wait for me? I turned around and you weren't there."

"You were looking at an ocellated turkey," I say. "I wanted to climb to the top."

Peter turns a full circle on the flat top of *El Mundo Perdido*. The tip top of Temple of the Giant Jaguar shoots up above the canopy, like a headstone rising toward the sun. "It's not much of a jungle."

It's not like those twisting green ferns and vines in Thailand, trees so overgrown that they looked nothing like trees. They were poofy or conical and sometimes even obelisk-shaped, the kinds of bushes and trees where Sneetches live. And there was so much green in so many different shades that you felt stupid for just saying green. Like you were sub-literate or sub-imaginative. But the Guatemalan jungle below is diffuse and mossy and almost brown. *Verde y marrón.*

"You can't see any birds up here," Peter says. "You can't see anything but the tops of the trees."

I can see the shiny black top of Diego's head. He's guarding our backpacks so we wouldn't have to carry water and sunscreen and Off! mosquito repellant on our backs when we climbed those steep steps.

Peter plants his hands on his hips and shakes his head. "I can't believe I climbed all the way up here for this."

I am no Maya Queen.

SECURITY

Ten silver circles surround my left wrist.

"You'll want to take your bracelets off before going through the metal detector," the security agent told me. She was a short black woman with an enormous bust. I hoped she had children. I hoped she pulled her kids in towards that bust and held them tight.

"Actually, they don't come off," I said.

"How did you get them on?" Her photo badge said "Regina Johnson," and in her picture she smiled.

"I put them on when I was thirteen," I said. "And then I grew."

"Well, they're quite pretty," Regina said. "We'll probably have to wand you."

"That's okay," I said. "I'm used to it."

THE OTHER SIDE OF THE GULCH

Most tourists get to Tikal early, like sunrise, because the pyramids were built to be seen with the sun rising or setting or at some other perfect point in the sky. But it's hard to get there earlier than late morning, really, when you begin from Belize and eat breakfast first at that little café in San Ignacio, the one that's painted yellow and pink and has a three-legged dog sleeping outside.

"I'm calling him Franz," I said, and fed him a sausage link. A dance troupe of fleas hip-hopped on his head.

"That thing's mangy." Peter peered over the top of his Peterson's Field Guide. "I don't think you should feed it. As a matter of fact, I don't think you should name it."

That road from Belize to Tikal was a pretty slow go. Right after we crossed the border it was still paved and smooth. Alongside the road were swarms of lovely women with children on their hips—

not skinny American girl hips—and men wearing faded blue jeans and white T-shirts. They must've known that white cotton against their brown skin made them look like gods. The border crossing seemed to be the social hub of their town. Everyone was walking toward it or away from it, with kids and baskets and bags, and they talked and they waved and I imagined that around some corner where foreigners couldn't see, they sang and they danced, too. Not too many kilometers from all that, the road got rough. The potholes were as large as watermelons—not nicely cut up into sweet, juicy wedges, like they sell from rickety tables along the streets of San Ignacio, but whole, like ripe big bombs—and there were so many of them, so close together, that they were difficult to avoid.

I had wanted to take a bus from our hotel in San Ignacio to the border, then after we crossed into Guatemala take a taxi to Tikal. Peter was worried about banditos, both on the road and in our taxi, so we paid seventy-five American dollars each for Gilberto to drive us in the white, air-conditioned mini-van with the hotel's logo on the side ("The Only Jungle in Town!"). I didn't mind so much, since it meant we were supporting the local economy, but I was pretty sure Gilberto wasn't getting paid that whole seventy-five dollars. It's too bad. He really knew a lot about the history and flora and fauna. And the birds.

The only way for Gilberto to avoid the watermelons in the road was to drive on the side of the road, in the gulch, and because the road was narrow and sloped, Gilberto drove very slowly, and because this road was narrow and sloped, our mini-van tilted mostly sideways. I thought we might tip over—especially when we stopped to look at an oriole or a heron, which I swore we have in the United States—but Peter explained to me the physics of why we wouldn't tip over. I nodded and said, "Yes, of course. That makes sense," but I still thought we might tumble to the other side of the gulch.

Like a Song

Dad and Janet got married when I was thirteen. They went to Thailand for their honeymoon, and invited me along. "This isn't just the beginning of our marriage," Janet said. "It's the beginning of our family."

One day Dad and I got lost in the Chatuchak Market in Bangkok, and that's not some metaphor. We were really lost, really had no idea how to find our way back to the street that would return us to our hotel. But the sky was still light and we had plenty of money and plenty of mango, and Janet was getting a massage for six American dollars and wouldn't be worried.

The silver bangles sat on a dingy white cloth on top of a table, shiny in the afternoon sun. An old Thai man was asleep in a chair. His arms were folded across his stomach and his chin rested on his chest. I slipped one bracelet over my little wrist and I liked how it looked, so I slipped on another. Those two looked so lonely alone, so I put on another, and with three there was a light clinking sound. I added another thin band of silver, and another delicately carved, and kept adding them until there were ten and they sang when I moved my arm.

My dad said something to the sleeping man, something in Thai that probably meant "Wake up!" but even more polite, because that's Dad's way.

The man woke and smiled with brown teeth. "How much?" my dad asked and pointed to my wrist, and the man said something and Dad said, "That seems like a lot," and the man said something else, and Dad said, "That seems like a bit too much, too," and the man said something else, and Dad smiled. "That seems about right."

When we found our way back to the hotel, Janet was pliable and smooth. Her long red hair fell in rings around her shoulders. She had the kind of curls you could tug on and they'd bounce right back.

I held up my arm for her to see. The bracelets clinked against each other as they fell toward my elbow. "Oh, aren't those pretty?" Janet said. "They sound like a song."

Human Sacrifices

I always figured it was a big honor to be sacrificed to the gods. You had to be pure and good and valued. Your family and friends would cry, but they'd be happy, too, because your sacrifice was for the greater good of your people.

Diego, our tour guide, says that's not always the way it went. The ancient Maya often offered up those who were weak or ill or of no use for the Kingdom of Tikal. Sometimes they were sacrificed just because they lost a game of basketball. It seems like a disrespectful way to treat the gods, giving them your rejects.

Peter's finally stopped panting from his one-hundred-and-five-foot climb. "I saw a limpkin," he says. "Guess where I saw it?"

"In a tree?" I ask.

"Limpkins don't hang out in trees," Peter says. "They're marsh birds."

"Okay, at a marsh?" I look over the side of the temple. It's a long drop down. In America, the lawyers would never let you climb something this high, something this strenuous. They'd have you sign all sorts of waivers before you did. If you fell or got pushed off one of these things, you'd probably die.

"I hope I see a keel-billed toucan," Peter says. "Or a Montezuma oropendula. They even spotted an orange-breasted falcon here last year."

"I want to see a jaguar." I bet jaguars eat Montezuma oropendulas for snacks. And they must be crazy about ocellated turkeys. On Thanksgiving I always make a little plate for Oliver, my cat, to eat along with me. I've tried feeding him green beans and cranberry sauce and whipped sweet potatoes and oyster stuffing—he nibbled at the stuffing once—but he'll only eat dark turkey meat and pumpkin pie with whipped cream. If Oliver likes his Thanksgiving plate so much, I bet a jaguar would devour an ocellated turkey.

"Jaguars are nocturnal," Peter says. "The only place you'll see one is at the zoo."

It sure is a long way down.

TAILOR MADE

Regina and I stood in the individual security inspection area. It was like a small closet or dressing room, but made out of some see-through plastic. Like plexiglass, but maybe bulletproof. Plexiglass probably isn't bulletproof. It's barely hockey puck proof.

Regina said, "Okay, dear. Please hold your arms out to your side."

I spread my wings wide, like the phoenix. My bracelets sang. Regina passed the wand over my torso, past my ribs. Twelve on each side, one floating. Janet's doctor told me that. The wand beeped over the back of my bra.

Peter stood outside the bulletproof dressing room. He said to Regina, "I told her not to wear those things through security. I told her they'd just slow everything down. They get in her way all the time. She should just cut them off." Except in order to be heard through the bulletproof plastic, he was kind of yelling.

"Spread your legs a little," Regina said.

With my legs in a triangle and my arms out to the side, I was ready to launch into a cartwheel. I could be some acrobatic superhero who fought her enemies using gymnastics. A cartwheel would be a double kick to someone's head and sternum, and a back flip would do even more serious damage. A somersault would be more of an evasive maneuver. I would never do a somersault on Regina.

Peter dropped his backpack to the floor. Then he picked it up again and made a big deal out of shifting it around, then dropped it to the floor. He checked his watch and looked side-to-side. "It's her bracelets," he said to a white-haired couple who were checking me out in the bulletproof dressing room.

Regina held the wand at the outside of my hip and ran it all the way down my pant leg to my ankle. Then she moved the wand to the inside of my pant legs, and carried it up my inseam to my crotch.

"Just a little break in the cuff," I said.

"For Christsake, Laurie," Peter yelled into the bulletproof dressing room. "Don't make jokes, this isn't funny."

"I thought it was funny." Regina stood. "And, sir, I'll ask you not to take the Good Lord's name in vain." She patted me on the shoulder. "You're all set, dear. Have a nice trip."

"Thanks, Regina," I said. "Have a good day."

Peter walked quickly toward our gate. I walked quickly to keep up. "Why did you call her Regina?" he asked.

"It's her name."

"What's that supposed to mean?" he said.

Everything Means Something

There were only two tour guides left by the time we arrived in Tikal. I expected them to be standing against a wall like the last two kids picked in a game of dodgeball. Maybe they'd jump up and down, with their hands high in the sky, yelling, "Pick me! Pick me! Pick me!" but they'd say Pick me! in Spanish instead. But the last two tour guides left in Tikal sat at a small table together, speaking rapid-fire Spanish and drinking glasses of juice oranger than orange juice.

Peter marched up to their table. "Do you both speak English?"

"Yes," they said in unison.

"Okay, you." Peter nodded to the taller looking one of the two. I knew he would.

Our tour guide picked up his backpack and said *adios* and *buena suerte* to his friend drinking juice that was oranger than orange juice.

"*Hola,*" I said to our tour guide. "*Como se llama usted?*"

"*Me llamo Diego,*" he said. He was about the same age as Peter, which was just a few years older than me. I wondered if, between classes, Peter ever sat around with his colleagues and drank fresh fruit juice. "*Y usted?*"

"*Laurie.*"

"What does it mean?" he asked, still in Spanish.

"It doesn't mean anything." Then I had to switch to English. "Where I come from, names don't mean anything."

"Sure they do," he said. "Everything means something. Even where you come from."

WISPS ON VALENTINE'S DAY

This morning in San Ignacio, the phone in our hotel room rang at 7:30. I picked it up and said, "*Hola?*" even though everyone speaks English in Belize.

"*Buenos dias!*" Dad said.

"*Buenos dias,*" I said. "*Como estas?*"

"*Bien, gracias. Y tu?*"

"*Bien,*" I said. Peter was in the shower, which was a good place for him to be. He hated it when Dad and I spoke other languages in front of him. It made him feel left out, like Dad and I had our own private language, and that language was Spanish or Italian or Thai.

"Happy Valentine's Day," Dad said. "Did you unwrap your book yet?" Dad always bought me a book for Valentine's Day, ever since I was old enough to open a book, to see all those words playing on the page. Sometimes they chased each other like tag, and other times they played hide-and-seek. I liked it best when they played leap frog.

"I'm saving it until tonight," I said. "We're going to Tikal today. Do you think it's weird that Peter's showering before we spend a day climbing ruins in the jungle?"

"I don't know," Dad said. "But he is a physicist. So, what's it like there this morning?"

"Sunny," I said. "We slept with the windows open, it was so cool all night. And in the middle of the night, there was this weird, loud noise. This crazy animal sound."

"Was it a howler monkey?"

"I don't think so." I tried to make the noise for Dad, which was a cross between an orangutan and a lion and a heron. Then I said, "Can I talk to Janet? I want to wish her a happy Valentine's Day."

"She's still sleeping." I wished there was some sound, then, a monkey howling or my bracelets singing or a security wand beeping. Something more than Peter's shower shhhhing, and Dad not breathing. "She decided to stop the chemo," he said. "Twice is enough."

"I just bought her a new scarf." Blue and gold. Like royalty. "And some new earrings."

"She's tired," he said. "Of it all."

"It's a nice heavy Guatemalan cloth," I said. "I thought it would be good for winter."

"She'll love the scarf," Dad said. "And the earrings, too."

When Peter came out of the shower his blond hair was wet and combed back, like freshly raked sand. They raked the sand like that on beaches of the Belizean *cayes*. Tangled mangrove washed up throughout the night, throughout the day, and Belizean workers raked it away. All day long, they just raked, raked, raked.

"Janet's stopping the chemo," I said. I hooked a finger through my bracelets and pulled hard, so those thin wires, all ten of them, made hot indents in my skin.

Peter sat on the woven red bedspread and pulled me into his arms. He held me against his chest and kissed my head. His lips were like butterflies in the wisps of my hair.

A Sloshy Swim

Gilberto suggests we have something cold to drink before getting into our air-conditioned mini-van and dodging more watermelons on the road back to Belize. He especially recommends the frozen limeade made with fizzy water. The drinks arrive on our table after fifteen minutes ("How long does it take to make a fucking limeade?" Peter asks) in giant margarita glasses, sloshy bright green and ice cold. The glass is so big and the straw is so long that I'm like Alice in Wonderland after she drinks the drink that says "Drink Me." If I could get that small I'd jump in and swim through the lime slush. I'd look up as I backstroke from green side to green side, and I'd sing some little song to the blue sky. I don't know what song it would be, but it would be in Spanish or Italian or Thai.

"We should stay overnight," I say. "We could watch the sun set, and the sun rise over the Acropolis." I don't know why it's called that. It doesn't sound like a Mayan word. It sounds like a Greek word. But maybe it's just an archeologist's word. "We could stay in one of the inns here, or find a motel in Flores."

"Overnight?" Peter says. "We don't have any clothes, or a toothbrush."

"We can rinse our clothes in the sink." Or at the side of a river, like the women we saw when we were driving here. The ones with children on their hips. "We can find a market and buy some toothpaste."

"How would we get back?" Peter says. "Gilberto's leaving in half an hour."

"We'll take a bus, or a taxi."

"But we already paid all that money for Gilberto to drive us here," he says. "And we're paying for our room back in San Ignacio. It's a waste of money."

Of course it is. Everything Peter's saying is quite logical. I know perfectly well that I'm being irrational. Impulsive.

"The next time we come to Central America we'll plan it so we spend the night here," Peter says.

"People always say that," I say. "They always say next time. But how often do you really go back to a place? I said that I'd go back to New Orleans. I said I'd go back and take that cemetery tour. And I'd eat beignets at Café Du Monde every day, instead of just once because I was worried about gaining weight, and I'd visit a few haunted houses, and I'd throw marshmallows to the alligators. I said that, and never did it, and now I never can."

Peter stirs the sloshy green with his straw. He's examining it like there's something suspicious in there. Or maybe he's just trying to determine its physical properties. "You're saying that you want to spend the night here because you think a hurricane is going to wash away Tikal?"

"Of course not." This city has been here for over two thousand years, even when it was buried under mounds of dirt and moss, and one of the great mysteries is why the Maya built a town nowhere near water. So a hurricane is unlikely. But you'd think that, as a physicist, Peter would understand that sometimes what you can't possibly imagine happening is the thing most likely to occur.

FATHER GUIDO SARDUCCI

Diego spoke English better than most Americans, with an accent dark and thick like shade-grown coffee. It reminded me of Father Guido Sarducci, especially when Diego said "pre-Columbian," although I don't think Father Guido Sarducci ever said pre-Columbian. Even though his English was good, I tried to speak Spanish to Diego anyway, since it was Guatemala and all.

"The pyramid of *El Mundo Perdido* is the oldest temple in Tikal," Diego said. "It's the only one built for purely astronomical purposes." He pointed to a high mossy hill across from it. "Underneath that hill is an unexcavated temple. There are still dozens, maybe hundreds just like it in the park, but there aren't enough resources to uncover them all."

That would make me crazy if I was an archeologist, knowing there was so much majestic beauty hidden under dirt and brush, but I couldn't get to it because there wasn't enough money. But archeologists are patient like that. They can divide a small square of land into smaller squares and use tiny brushes to whisk the dust away. Maybe they'll find a bone or a chip from a vase. Maybe they'll find nothing at all.

Diego looked around. "Where's your husband?"

"He's not my husband," I said in Spanish. "He's looking at an ocellated turkey." Except I didn't know how to say "ocellated turkey" in Spanish. "*Como se dice* ocellated turkey *en espanol?*"

"*Pavo ocelado.*" Diego pointed up. "Are you going to climb to the top?"

The top was distant and flat. "I thought it would be more romantic."

"*El Mundo Perdido?*"

"No," I said. "Valentine's Day."

"Oh, I don't celebrate Valentine's Day."

I turned away from the flat top pyramid. Diego's eyes were also like coffee, the kind you have after dinner with a slice of double chocolate torte and ripe raspberries. "I think it's an American holiday," I said.

"It's not that," Diego said. "I don't celebrate because I don't have a lover." When he said *lover*, he sounded nothing like Father Guido Sarducci.

IT WAS OUR FIRST TIME

Peter ran his fingers over my bracelets. Up and down. Ding, ding, ding. Ching, ching, ching. "I liked hearing them when we were making love."

"Mmmm." It was from someplace much deeper than the back of my throat. His blond chest hair was soft under my cheek. Chest hair on a man was usually more coarse. The only place on a man with hair so soft was at the base of his spine, in that small indent in his back. That's the place where cashmere comes from.

Peter circled my wrist with his thumb and forefinger. "They don't come off, do they?"

"No," I said. "Not anymore."

"Where did you get them?"

"In Thailand." I wondered if Peter would stay the night. Not many did. Most had early morning meetings. So many men had early morning meetings that you'd think that the streets were teeming with testosterone at six a.m. "When Dad and Janet got married we all went there together."

"Janet's not your mother?" Janet had met Peter before I did, at a cocktail party welcoming new faculty to Dad's school last fall. I had helped her get ready that night. She wore a new silk scarf, orange with hot pink paisleys. She wasn't interested in wigs. A colorful scarf and some dangly earrings would do her just fine.

"My mother died in a car accident when I was three," I said.

"I'm sorry." Peter closed his eyes, settled against my pillow.

"It's okay." His chest hair tickled my lips. "I never knew her."

VAMANOS!

"Are you sure?" Gilberto asks me. He's speaking in Spanish. Everyone's figured out by now that Peter doesn't speak Spanish, so they're all talking to me that way. They don't seem to understand that I'm not going to tell them anything I haven't told Peter, whether it's in Spanish, English, or gobbledygook.

"I'm sure," I tell Gilberto. "I'll be fine. Really. You just drive safely."

"*Bien.*" Gilberto nods to the ground solemnly. "*Adios, senorita. Buena suerte.*"

Of course, I'll see Gilberto again tomorrow, back at the hotel, after I take a taxi to the border and a bus to San Ignacio. I wonder if I'll see Peter there, too. If he'll stay. He really should. Tonight he should shave and shower—even though he already did this morning—and put on his white Bermuda shorts with that pale blue T-shirt that brings out his eyes, and he should go down onto the main street and eat tacos and drink Belikin, the local beer, and he should chat up a beautiful Belizean woman with dark brown skin. He should buy her peppermint ice cream and dance with her in the street, and then take her back to the hotel and make love to her with the windows open so the animals can howl all night. And after that, we'll see.

I wave goodbye as the dust behind the van floats my way. When it's out of sight, Diego stands next to me. "The sun will set in about an hour. Would you like to watch it from the top of *El Mundo Perdido?*"

"*Si.*" I pick up my backpack. The corner of the unwrapped book pokes at my spine. Just a little. Just like it's saying hi. I look at Diego. I say, "*Vamanos.*"

cool dry ice

The Valium that Caroline swallowed on the way to LaGuardia started to dim high above the Colorado plains. It was an accident that the effects were abating just in time for her layover. She had taken the pill in the cab, stuck in traffic. The initial shock of her father's death had worn off, and she needed something else to take its place. With the details of planning a cremation, a memorial, a reception behind her, her mind might hone in on the loss. Caroline had no desire to grieve in the backseat of a Yellow Cab.

Her plane descended toward dusty flatlands. The Rockies were so far from the airport that it didn't seem like they belonged to the same place. The cragged mountains were one thing, the brown plains another. The airport roof was dozens of giant peaks made from fabric pulled into tight white cones. They were supposed to look like snow-capped mountains, but to Caroline they were more like hazmat tents vaulted side-by-side.

This was the second time she'd seen Kort on a layover in Denver. The first time was a month earlier, when she was traveling for work. They drove to the far-away foothills and sat on red rocks, watching the city lights and stars compete for first prize. With her dress pushed up and his jeans pulled down, Caroline and Kort burned brighter than all that filament and fusion.

The landing was bumpy, or maybe it was the Valium wearing off. Caroline closed her eyes and pulled at her seatbelt while the brakes and engines screamed. She had two hours before her connecting flight to L.A., so there was only enough time for drinks and maybe one appetizer, depending on how long it would take to get to the main terminal. That was another thing that 9/11 screwed up—on a layover, your friends could no longer meet you at your gate and sit in the bar and drink Bloody Marys while you watched planes lift away. They used to hug you goodbye right before you boarded the plane, and all that would still be with you, on the plane, as you inserted the silver belt buckle into the latch. Now you had to leave a secured area to meet your friends, which meant long treks and moving walkways and trains. Most of the time, Caroline didn't bother.

At the end of the moving walkway was the women's bathroom. It doubled as a tornado shelter—a yellow sign said so. She imagined dozens of women crouched down on the floor while cyclones tore off the snow-capped peaks. Caroline peed, checked her hair, fixed her lipstick. The fluorescent lights made her skin red and her hair green. She realized this is how she would look if she died in a tornado. They would peel away the tight white fabric molded to her body and yell, *We have one with green hair!*

Caroline left the tornado shelter and rode two escalators to wait for the train. When it arrived, bells rang. Not like church bells; more like sleigh bells. People streamed out, people streamed in. The tunnel was dark and the train went fast. Caroline wanted it to go so fast that the steel cars hit the cement walls, chasing sparks through the tunnel like lightning bugs.

When the train doors opened, she rode two up-escalators that deposited her under the bright white peaks. Caroline saw a mother with three kids and a girl holding a rose and a chauffeur in a badly fitting suit. There was a fountain and rental car kiosks and deafening ambient airport noise, but no Kort.

She reached for her cell phone, and then she heard it above the din: slap, slap, slap, slap.

Boots against linoleum. His blond hair was loose, and his white shirt swayed. She held up a hand, and thought maybe he smiled.

"Sorry I'm late," Kort said. "Traffic was a bitch."

Kort looked like he had left part of himself back there, in the asphalt freeway jam. His cheekbones were too sharp and his under-eyes too dark and his jeans too loose. He hadn't shaved and she wasn't sure he had bothered to shower, either.

"Damn, you're quite the sight for sore eyes," he said, although she thought it unlikely. She was the sight of sore eyes, sore lungs, sore heart.

"So, where can we get a drink?" Caroline's smile hurt. "I have less than two hours."

Up two more escalators was the bar with a smoking lounge. Kort had quit three years earlier, but didn't mind that Caroline smoked. You couldn't mind other people smoking if you wanted to be a gigging musician. Caroline ordered a martini, very dry, and Kort got a scotch, neat. She lit a cigarette and blew smoke to the side. It made her squint, or maybe it was staring at him that made her eyes tilt like Venetian blinds. "So, what's with this ravaged look?" she said.

"That took you a whole ten minutes," Kort said. "You're losing your touch, Car."

"It's just that heroin-chic went out years ago, baby." If she'd seen his face two weeks earlier, she would have said he looked "ashen." But ashes were different to her now. They were grittier. Multi-hued. Heavy in her hand.

She knew they wouldn't talk, really talk, until they drank, and so they drank. The bar was brown—walls, tables, chairs, air. It's like someone knew better than to paint the room white. It was probably the same reason the airport was so far from downtown Denver, from the bulging band of smog. The architects knew that the airport's high white peaks would scar with sludge. Not right away—it takes years for that color to deposit so thick it can't be scraped away.

"So, how was it?" Kort asked. "Better or worse than you expected?"

"Different," she said. They'd speculated about their father's deaths before. Kort doubted he'd shed one tear when his alcoholic father finally succumbed to the host of degenerative diseases awaiting him. Caroline figured that when her father died, she'd feel an easing in her chest, like more air slowly being let in. But she was surprised at the resonance of her moans when her brother called to tell her Dad was gone. She sounded like an orangutan, aching for his mate. Five days later, she was just tired.

"Did your brother help?" Kort asked.

She shook her head. "Totally shut down. I'm running around Brooklyn trying to plan a fucking funeral, and he's sleeping until three in the afternoon." *We're going to make all the decisions together,* her brother said on her first day there. *It's just you and me now.* But the grief and the mania and the depression were too potent a cocktail for him. It kept him pinned to his bed.

Kort's glass was empty, and new drinks were set on the table. His looked like liquid caramel. Caroline's was how dry ice would look, if dry ice could melt. She wanted to suck liquid caramel into her veins and let it flow slow, thick, through her. "So, how are you?" she asked. "Any better?"

Kort shook his head. "I've fucked everything up here."

A month ago in the foothills—the night with the filament and fusion—Kort had told her why his girlfriend left him. "*You're going to laugh,*" he had said. "*It's a goddamn soap opera.*" Caroline promised him, "*I won't laugh,*" so he laid it out, how he was caught in bed with another woman, his boxers on the floor. "*I actually stood in the street screaming, 'Don't leave me!' as she drove away,*" Kort told her. Caroline couldn't help herself, then—she laughed. He laughed too, and it was about that time that his lips found hers.

"All the stupid shit I've done . . . ." Kort's eyes were heavy, a void that pulled everything in, let nothing out. "I can't even look myself in the mirror."

She'd seen a vacuum in his eyes before, but not this dense. Sometimes the cause was tangible: girl troubles, band troubles, a visit from his father. She would crawl into bed next to him—but not with him—and place a hand on his back and talk about nothing. That was usually enough to keep him from being sucked in, away. But it wasn't just him that needed to be pulled in this time. She couldn't imagine what they looked like: two objects tethered to each other, but grounded in nothing.

"Move back to L.A.," she said.

Kort laughed in a way that sounded like a hundred separate pin-pricks. "Running away isn't going to fix what I did."

"Do you remember what you said when you told me you were moving?" It was his birthday six months earlier, and there had been pot and vodka and something else, something the color of strawberries that swirled inside Caroline's head. "You said you were leaving L.A. to find moral clarity." He actually said those words. "And now you're telling me this is what you've found?"

Kort reached across the table and pinched the cigarette between Caroline's lips. He put it between his, covering her lipstick stain. She hoped it would stain him, his lips, his blood, long after he gave the cigarette back. He blew out smoke. "I must've been high," he said. "To say something like that."

He leaned back across the table and held the cigarette toward Caroline. She parted her lips for him. "Stay the night," he said. "Let's get out of here."

If there was anyone who could get her out of here, it would be Kort, and she could get him out, too, and they'd climb on his motorcycle and ride into the mountains and stand on a cliff where they'd look at the fake white peaks a hundred miles away. They'd dive off the edge together, and float through the dry ice fog.

"I have a meeting in L.A. tomorrow morning," she said.

"Move it."

"Maybe someday, when I'm the big boss, I'll be able to rearrange meetings just for you." Caroline's cigarette crackled bitter orange. "But for now, I have to show up."

Kort leaned back with a thud that almost knocked over his chair. "Jesus, Car. Why am I even here?"

"What do you think? That we'll fuck and everything will be better?"

Maybe it would be, for at least a few minutes during and a few minutes after, and those few minutes would be worth something. But Kort and Caroline didn't have fucking kind of sex. They didn't have making love kind of sex, either; they had something which floated in between. Caroline needed something more than in between, something she could either hold onto or toss away.

"That's what you think?" Kort asked. "That I came out here to get laid?"

"I'm hoping you came out here because we're friends." It was Unspoken Rule #1: The friendship always comes first. Sex is Monopoly money, plentiful and easy to steal. But the thing that makes it work, that makes it more than a fuck and less than love, that's a green grain of sand.

"Maybe we should change that," he said.

"Oh, so you don't want to be friends anymore?"

"I mean that maybe we should try being something more than good friends who occasionally go to bed."

They had tried that once, long ago. At least, they'd been on the precipice of trying, and then realized the only thing below was a sharp fall. *You'll last much longer as a friend than a girlfriend,* Kort had said to her then.

Caroline crushed her cigarette into the ashtray between them. "That's so pathetic."

Kort snorted. "Us trying for something serious is pathetic? Thank you very much."

"It's pathetic because you're in love with another girl and you miss her and you're so lonely you can't stand to live inside your own skin." He was grasping at whatever gossamer threads seemed familiar, hoping they'd stop his freefall through space. "It has nothing to do with me."

"I'm not sure which one of us you underestimate more," he said.

It wasn't that she underestimated either of them. She knew exactly what and who they both were and the weight of the baggage they carried. Hers had just gotten heavier, more unwieldy. The scales were unfairly tipped now.

"I have to go," she said.

"It's only been an hour."

"The lines are long, and there's that stupid train . . . ." Escalators and moving walkways and tornado shelters. "If I don't get there early they'll think I'm a terrorist." She stood and pulled on the handle of her carry-on bag.

Kort reached into his back pocket. "Okay, let me—"

"It's on me." She threw two twenties on the table.

"—walk you down."

They walked in silence, even though she wanted to talk and was sure he did, too, but that ambient airport noise was too damn loud. They got on the escalator, Caroline and her bag on one step, and Kort behind her on another. They were skiers on a slope, gliding down. Then he put his arms around her. His hands were hot at the base of her throat.

At the bottom of the escalator was another escalator, and at the bottom of that were ribbons of black tape snaking toward security gates. Kort moved his hands to Caroline's waist and she twisted so they were face-to-face.

"There's something I'm supposed to say," he said. "Before you leave."

"No," she said. "There's really not." That would require Kort knowing what he wanted, and he didn't. He couldn't. Not that Caroline knew what she wanted either, but that was Rule #2: Someone had to at least pretend to know what to do.

She turned and slid down, down, down, but the slopes weren't so slick or so soft, and the soles of her feet hurt when she hit the floor. She looked back to the top, into the apex of a great white peak. Kort was walking away. His blond hair was loose, and his white shirt swayed.

Inside the tornado shelter Caroline opened her carry-on bag. Inside was her makeup case, and inside her makeup case were the pills with mysterious letters and numbers engraved on their bellies. You couldn't speak their names, you had to know the code. She crushed a white one—OC 40—and swallowed the powder with water from the bathroom sink. Tornado water, she thought. It was the only way to clear the debris.

Caroline's silver buckle was latched, and she bathed in the OxyContin calm. The plane lurched toward the sky. It was amazing that something as light as air could lift something as dense as steel and make it float, make it soar. Caroline glided past towers of steel and glass, piercing through Denver's band of smog. She was suspended between the brown cloud and the gossamer ether, and she could see it all: plains carpeted with corn stalks and clotheslines stretching all the way to New York, and west of the Great Divide the land rose and fell and fell and rose until it dropped into the sea. Straight below, Caroline was perched on the edge of a great white peak. She stood with a handful of ash, ready to dive into the cool dry ice.

riding to the shore

Ginny stood on the counter of the diner decorated in tinfoil.
She's my wife, if you want to call her that, which I do. She'd
made bracelets and earrings and a fake-fancy necklace by folding and
shaping tiny glinting pieces. She even made a tinfoil tiara, perched on
her red wig from the chemo clinic. Ginny clasped a ketchup bottle to
her chest. "I really didn't expect to win," she gushed. "It's such an
honor to even be nominated. I have so many people to thank."

"Get your skinny ass down from there and get back to work," Joe
said. He was standing over the flattop cooking us all some eggs.
"Deb, get your honey's skinny ass down from there before she breaks
a leg," he said to me.

I didn't care about getting Ginny's skinny ass down from there.
She looked too damn pretty being all silly and shiny, like she used to
be before she got sick. Her only customer at her only table was
laughing his ass off anyway, and everyone else was home watching
the Oscars. It didn't matter if you lived six hundred miles from
Hollywood. People still acted like all that business mattered.

"And really," Ginny said. "There's someone who deserves this
award more than me, and that's my high school drama teacher, Mrs.
Futtlebutt. Mrs. Futtlebutt, will you please join me on stage?" She
extended a hand down to me with a dopey look in her eyes.

"Oh my," I said, clutching my throat. "What an honor." I grabbed
the edge of the counter to steady myself, then crawled up next to

Ginny's tennis shoes. The Formica was hard on my knees and my knees were hard on me, so I pushed myself the rest of the way up fast. Nobody could accuse me of being young and graceful, that's for damn sure.

Ginny handed me the ketchup bottle. "Mrs. Futtlebutt, this is for you." She placed the tinfoil tiara on my head.

"You sure are a couple of silly broads." Joe stood there holding plates of fried eggs and hash browns. "Now get down before your dinner gets cold."

We helped each other down. Ginny wiped off the counter with a rag, just like she did a dozen times a day, and we slid into a booth with Joe. I put Tabasco and ketchup on my eggs, but Ginny ate hers plain. That's about all her stomach could handle these days.

When the phone rang, Ginny got up to answer it. "Eureka Diner, Home of the World's Best Eggs, Crafted by Joe the Master Chef. How can I assist you this evening?"

"Wish she'd stop answering like that," Joe said through a mouth of hash browns. I knew he didn't really mean it—there's just no way anybody could.

Ginny screamed. Not in a scary way, but more like she was at a Beatles concert. "No, really?" she said into the phone. "When? For how long? . . . Oh, I can't wait! I love you!"

"Got competition, Deb?" Joe elbowed me in the ribs.

"Ha, ha." There was only one other person Ginny said *I love you* to: her daughter.

Ginny slid back into the booth. "You'll never guess what?"

"Christy coming to visit?" I said into my runny yolks.

"Yes! Tomorrow. She's driving up first thing in the morning."

Christy used to come stay with us for a week in April and another at Christmas and for six long ones in the summer. That was before she turned eighteen, when she still had to do what the custody agreement said. Too bad that agreement said nothing about looking me in the eyes, or saying anything more than "Let me talk to my mom" when she called, which wasn't real often. Not since Ginny got sick. Not since I was left to handle it all.

After Ginny's shift was done, we went straight home. We brushed our teeth side by side, taking turns spitting in the sink and passing the water cup to rinse. The sink was only a couple feet from the toilet which was only a couple feet from the bathtub—everything was only a couple feet from each other—but we knew how to make it work. We'd even figured it out with Ginny kneeling in front of the toilet and no room for me behind her. I could sit in the bathtub and reach one hand over to Ginny's back to try and cool it off.

We got in bed under the wedding quilt my brother Keith gave us. Ginny curled onto her side, and I curved around her back. I put my hand on Ginny's stomach. I didn't rub, because that could be too much for her sometimes. But she liked a little pressure there. A little warmth.

"You should sleep in tomorrow," I said. She didn't have to be at work until eleven—Joe was real good about letting her work short shifts.

"I might go in early," she said. "See if I can catch part of breakfast and pick up some extra tips."

Maybe it seemed like Ginny should save her energy, but it was so good when she got it that she used it right up. I didn't blame her. The energy surged in waves, and when a pretty one came along, she just had to jump on and ride it to the shore.

Ginny turned toward me, leaving a space just big enough for her to lay a hand on one of my breasts. She traced my nipple with her fingers, traced it like you run a finger through soft sand. That might have been all, just Ginny tracing my nipple because she often wasn't up for much more, but my nipple got hard and I felt myself going warm and wet. I ran my hand from Ginny's ass up to her head. Ginny moaned when I got to her smooth scalp. It turned out there were lots of nerve endings up there, and it felt good to Ginny in a way neither of us had known about before the chemo. Even though Ginny was in remission and her hair could grow back, she kept on shaving her head and wearing that silly wig.

Ginny slid her hand off my breast and travelled down to my stomach, and when her hand was there, on my stomach, I hoped that my healthy insides would soak into Ginny's palm and make their way back inside of her. Even though some of her stomach had got cut out, I figured there was still a way for her to be whole. Her hand kept sliding down and between, and then it was less about Ginny's hand and more about her fingers.

She'd caught a pretty wave and we were going to ride it to the shore.

I once saw a movie about three girls who were maids at a resort. They'd go into a room together and talk about boys and surfing while they stripped beds and folded towels and wiped down sinks. But I worked alone at the motel, pushing my cart from room to room.

I knocked on a first-floor door. "Housekeeping," I said, even though there was probably no one to hear. Most people only slept in Eureka for one night on their way to or from the Redwoods. By the time I got to a room, the sheets were heaped and the towels were damp, the trash nothing more than a strand of dental floss or a dirty Band-Aid.

The inside of the room looked like a ghost town, with pages of the *Times-Standard* scattered over the floor. A pink lipstick stain rimmed a plastic cup next to the bed. I went about changing sheets and scrubbing the toilet and vacuuming the floor. It was the kind of job you didn't need to think much for, which was good last fall. I'd been too worried that the surgery didn't get all of Ginny's tumor and that the chemo might not get the rest. Maybe a job that didn't keep me on my middle-aged feet all day would have been nice, but at least it forced me upright. Made me move.

A shiny gum wrapper in the trash made me think of Ginny standing on the counter the night before. She used to be silly like that all the time. Her husband sometimes left her in charge of the market in Fresno while he ran to the bank or a meeting. As soon as he left, Ginny'd take over the P.A. system. "Knock, knock?" she'd say to the entire store.

"Who's there?" I'd yell from the floor.

"Interrupting sheep," she'd say.

"Interrupting shee—"

"Baaaaa!"

At least once a week Ginny brought in food for the employees, Rice Krispies squares or chocolate pretzels or pumpkin-shaped cookies. She didn't mind pitching in, either. Once a customer spilled a bag of rice on Aisle 6, and a kid threw up on Aisle 4. Ginny rolled a bucket and mop out to 4, and didn't complain one bit while I swept up rice two aisles away.

◆ ◆ ◆

After work, I stopped by the diner to see if Ginny wanted anything special from the store. She had a couple of tables, so I sat at the counter with a bowl of clam chowder. There wasn't much lying around the kitchen that morning, so all I had for lunch was a hard-boiled egg, some saltines, and two slices of American cheese. I devoured the soup, not even chewing the bits of clam.

Three pencils stuck out from the curls of Ginny's red wig. The hospital had wigs people donated after their hair grew back or after they were gone. One day I came home to find Ginny lying on the couch with one hand on her belly, and this red bouffant wig on her head. "Joe's not gonna like it," I told her. "Well, then he can just kiss my grits," she said. Turned out that Joe got a kick out of the wig, and took to calling her Flo and fake-yelling that she was a silly broad.

Ginny wiped her hands on her apron and leaned toward me. "More coffee, babe?"

I shook my head. "Anything you want from the store?" What sounded good to Ginny changed from day to day, and there were some days when nothing did.

"Vanilla ice cream," Ginny said. "With little brown specks in it. And noodles. And peas."

I wrote it down on a piece of paper so I wouldn't forget. Anymore, it seemed if I didn't write something down, there wasn't much chance of me remembering.

"Holy shit!" Ginny said, and went for the door. Standing outside the front window was Christy, wearing jeans and a bright blue UCLA T-shirt. Her hair streamed long and blond down her back, like Ginny's used to.

Ginny started screaming—I could hear that from inside—and jumping up and down. She hugged Christy and it was hard to tell if Christy hugged back, because Ginny had pretty much pinned her arms.

"That's Gin's girl, huh?" Joe squinted toward the window.

"That's her," I said.

"She looks older."

"Don't we all." Not that Christy cared about how old I looked or felt. I was pretty sure that girl didn't care one bit how hard I'd had it, working full time and driving Ginny to the clinic, cooking and cleaning and wondering if there'd ever be fun again.

Ginny unpinned Christy and waved, then pointed to Christy like I might have missed the whole thing otherwise. It had been quite a while since I'd seen Ginny smile so wide for so long.

I cooked up noodles for dinner, with butter and peas, and figured we'd have vanilla bean ice cream for dessert. Christy took one bite of the noodles and said, "Kinda bland."

"Spices are next to the stove." Ginny pointed.

Christy walked to the drawer, which was only about an arm's length from the table. Before she'd tasted the noodles, I'd asked what classes she was taking, so Christy went right on about that. "Mostly, I'm knocking out core classes," she said, sprinkling on garlic salt. "But I've got this cool psych class on Theories of Cognition and Abnormal Behavior."

"That's quite a mouthful," I said.

"Cognition means the way people think about things." Christy stirred her noodles and sat back down. "And abnormal means—"

"I know what abnormal means." I'd taken a smattering of classes at Fresno Community College when I was Christy's age. Before it got to be too much, studying, working, paying the rent.

"You still a maid at that motel?" Christy asked. She had the same blue eyes as her mom, but they sure didn't see people the same way. "It sounds gross. Cleaning other people's toilets."

"There's much harder things than that," I said. That girl had never cleaned up after anyone a day in her life. She'd certainly never had to wipe up puke or mop up diarrhea that wouldn't go away.

"It sounds fun," Ginny said. "Learning about so many different things." She hadn't touched her noodles, but I didn't know if that was about the excitement of Christy being there, or more about her stomach.

"So, what's with the wig?" Christy asked through a full mouth.

"It's kind of fun, don't you think?" Ginny pushed and primped her curls like she was Rita Hayworth fussing to go on stage. She didn't normally wear the wig at home, at the dinner table. She usually wore a hat or a scarf or nothing at all, and when she wore nothing at all I would reach over and run a hand across her smooth head.

"It's weird," Christy said. "You can do better."

"So, what are you doing here?" I asked.

"Came to see my mom."

"Why now?"

"Well, it's spring bre—"

"No, why now?" I clanked down my fork. "Why now, when she's all finished with the surgery and the chemo, why are you coming to see her now, and you didn't then?"

"Deb," Ginny reached over to touch my hand, but all she got was a fist. "She was just starting college. I didn't want her to get distracted."

"That was your decision, huh?" I looked at Ginny, who was looking at her napkin trying to pretend that the hurt hadn't dug away at her. "What about Christmas break? Or Thanksgiving? Or just some long weekend."

"College is hard," Christy said. "It takes all my time."

It was the excuse Ginny had told me and herself and everyone else again and again, so you couldn't really blame Christy for falling back on it. But I wanted Christy to tell the truth. I want someone else to say that Ginny being sick was so terrifying you couldn't see or feel straight, that it made you want to hide away.

"You don't know one damn thing about hard," I said.

"Mom!" Christy's voice got loud and whiny. "Don't let her talk to me like that."

"Stop it," Ginny said. "Both of you stop it, stop it, stop it!" She pulled off her wig and threw it on the table between us. It sat there limp and dull, like a circus balloon that lost all its air.

I pushed my chair back and rose up tall. I picked up Ginny's wig from the kitchen table and took it with me, out the front door.

I walked for a long time. My legs and feet were already tired from pushing my cart from room to room all day, but there wasn't much else to do. I'd left the apartment without grabbing the car keys or my wallet, like some teenage drama queen. I didn't even grab a coat.

My head and hands were cold. I wanted to blame it on the moon, which couldn't even bother to get half-full. The cold light made the sequoias look like Halloween decorations, blackened cutouts from giant pieces of cardboard. I slipped Ginny's wig over my head. It was a tight fit and I had to yank it down hard.

After Ginny left Christy's dad, the last thing on her mind was being a wife again. She was plenty happy just to be making a home with me. But when they started marrying folks down in San Francisco a few years back, it just seemed like the thing to do. My brother, Keith, even said he'd come up from Fresno with a minister friend who'd do the ceremony for free.

We drove to San Francisco early in the morning and stood in line for nearly five hours. Everyone was laughing and holding hands, sharing coffee and muffins, and someone we didn't even know handed a single red rose to every couple in line. After we got our license, we took the trolley down to Fisherman's Wharf and had a glass of wine. We sat staring out at Alcatraz, wondering why someone would build something so ugly in the middle of so much pretty. When Ginny asked the waiter, he said, "They wanted the prisoners to see what they were missing." I know they were criminals, but it still seemed cruel, forcing them to look right at what they couldn't have every single day.

By the time Keith got to us, it was all over. He'd heard on the radio. No more marriage licenses were being given out, and the ones already out there didn't count. Keith said that didn't matter none, we should still do the ceremony. His minister friend blessed me and Ginny while we kissed and exchanged rings. The fog had come in, and we couldn't see past the bridge. Only the tops peeked through, and they didn't look golden so much as a ragged red.

I drove us home the next day, playing the radio to cut the quiet. The signal turned fuzzy about a mile into the Humbolt Redwoods. The giants made it dark like dusk in there, even though it was just past lunch. I looked over at Ginny to ask for a CD, but her eyes were closed. Her forehead rested against the window and her blond hair curled around her neck. Even in the daytime dusk, I could see the collar of Ginny's pink shirt was blotched by tears.

The red wig made my head hot and my scalp itch. I shifted it around, shoving strands of hair underneath, then pulling them back out. But there was no way to make it comfortable, so I took it off. I took off that wig and dropped it to the ground, and I stepped on it once or twice. Hard.

When I got home the living room was hot and bright. Christy was on the couch watching TV. "Where's your mom?" I asked.

"Gee, I don't know." Christy didn't move her eyes. "Maybe she's in the screening room or the conservatory or something." The girl had no intention of going for sorry, and I suppose I didn't either.

I pushed open the bedroom door real quiet. Ginny was lying on her side with a pillow scrunched underneath her. I unbuttoned my shirt and unhooked my bra, and while I was taking off my jeans, Ginny turned and watched. The sliver of moon peeking in the window made me feel flabby and ghost white. I pulled on Keith's flannel shirt, the one I'd been sleeping in since stealing it from him years ago. It was worn and ratty, but sure didn't feel that way.

"Where's my wig?" Ginny asked.

I got under the quilt, looked at the popcorn ceiling. The peaks and valleys looked like the far-away surface of the moon. "I lost it."

"What do you mean, you lost it?"

"I guess I dropped it," I said. "Out in the woods."

"How could you drop it?" Ginny sounded exhausted more than mad. "I need it. I wear it every day."

"Not every day."

There was as much room between us as could be in our double bed. I'd hate to see how we looked, like two sides of a log split by a dull axe.

"You were too hard on her," Ginny said.

"She doesn't respect me," I said. "Us."

Ginny turned to face me, and the lack of light didn't matter. I could see her blue eyes just fine, her sharp cheekbones, her thin lips, bare skull. "She thinks you're why I left her dad."

"That makes no sense." I could see how Christy thought that when her folks split up, because that's how young people think. But now she was in college, thinking for herself. She should have figured out it was more complicated. That a big piece of Ginny had already left him, long before I came along. That all of her was never really with him in the first place.

"She's the only family I've got," Ginny said. She had no brothers or sisters, and ten years had gone since her parents last talked to her. Ten years since Ginny decided she couldn't stay married to Christy's dad.

I reached across the small space between us. I slid my hand over Ginny's bare head. There was no wave between us that night, but no riptide either. There was just water creeping on the shore, and then draining back, leaving a blanket of smooth, wet sand.

The next day when I got home from work, Ginny and Christy weren't in front of the TV. They weren't in the kitchen, so I headed to the bedroom. I heard Christy before seeing her, heard her small, clipped whining sounds. She was on the ground next to the closed bathroom door, hands wrapped around her raised knees. Ginny was behind the door, retching up nothing but bitter bile. It used to be the tumor that made Ginny sick. Then it was the chemo. Anymore, it was because her stomach was so small it didn't empty out right. Her body knew purging would rid her of the pain.

Christy looked up at me, eyes puffy and pink. "She won't come out and won't let me in."

I crouched down next to her, the muscles around my knees straining like old rubber bands. "How long's she been in there?"

Christy wiped her nose with the back of her hand, her fist coming back wet and shiny. "I don't know. Like, half an hour, maybe."

I was still wearing my work uniform, brown polyester pants and a navy blue smock. I swiped the corner of the smock across Christy's nose. She was just a scared kid who didn't know how to deal with a sick mom. She shouldn't have to.

I reached above the door frame for the allen key. "It's just me, babe," I said to Ginny as I let myself in.

Her body was a limp paisley on the cool bathroom floor, her ear pressed down like an Indian listening for footsteps. "Close the door."

I pushed it most of the way closed but didn't let it latch, didn't let it lock. Left some room for Christy to hear, to talk, to move. I stepped into the tub and sat with my legs long. I reached my hand out to Ginny's back, to her green T-shirt damp with sweat.

"Someone left a brochure in one of the rooms," I said. "For Lake Shasta." Nobody ever left clues of where they were going, but sometimes I could piece together where they'd been. "Prettiest picture you'd ever seen, the water like a mirror. Same color as the sky."

"Was the mountain in it?" Ginny asked

"Oh, sure." I reached over and flushed the toilet, sucking away layers of bile. "The snow was so bright that it looked like it was covered in diamonds."

The bathroom door pushed open real quiet. Christy's voice had a shakiness that didn't match up with the girl from the kitchen table last night. "You okay, Mom?"

"Been better, been worse," Ginny said.

Christy couldn't get to her mom because there was no space to crouch into. It would have been easy for her to leave, to just close the door and let us be.

"Here." I folded my knees to my chest and scooted to the other end of the tub. Christy climbed in next to me. I lifted my hand off Ginny's sweat-stained shirt and nodded there, to the damp imprint of my palm on her back.

Christy reached toward Ginny real slow, like she was moving toward a fire. Her hand landed on my palm-mark. It seemed like Christy might jerk back, away. It was easy to get scared like that, like your hand might just make the pain worse. Like it might make the disease come back. Like it might be your fault in the first place. All that fear never really went away. It just kept shifting around, trying to figure out what else to be. But Christy kept her hand steady. Her mother's back. Next to me.

I kneeled up in the hard tub. I ran my hand over the landscape of Ginny's skull, over hills and rivers and flat sand beaches.

"This summer," I said, "We'll go over to Shasta. We'll get a room that looks out on the mountain." I got a discount at other motels in the chain and, maybe, if we started saving right away, there'd be enough for a couple of nights. "We'll rent a little boat and pack a picnic, and I'll row you out to the middle of the lake."

We'd have wine and vanilla bean ice cream, if that's what Ginny wanted that day. The two of us would lie back in the sun, letting our skin grow warm and wet in the middle of the lake.

"We'll take lots of pictures," I said. "Make one into a Christmas card."

"I'll put it up on my mirror," Christy said. "In my dorm."

I couldn't see it, Christy's dorm or her mirror or the Christmas card held on by clear tape. But I had no problems seeing Ginny lying in a boat caressed by the sun, the water like a mirror, and Mount Shasta glittering nearby.

my son's father

Give Jimmy a kiss for me," he says.
"When he wakes up." I finger the imaginary coils of a yellow phone cord, how it tangles into itself and can only be made straight again by spinning upside down.

"It's late." He says this as if I'm the one who called after midnight from a telescope aimed at the Incan sky. It's only two time zones away, but over four thousand miles south-by-southeast, and another six thousand straight up.

"Jimmy wishes . . ." My voice gets sucked away. My son is only three and I don't know if he wishes much. "He wishes he could see you."

"There's so much dust in Centaurus A," he says.

My son's father: worn motorcycle leather and gravitational math, praline ice cream on salt-chapped lips, tires grabbing hot asphalt through the sharp twists of the Pacific Coast curves.

minor league lessons

My grandmother floored the accelerator on the golf cart. It only had a top speed of twenty miles per hour, but I still clutched the edges of the vinyl seat. She aimed us toward the front doors of Anasazi Meadows, where her fellow residents were being helped into a minivan amid a quagmire of walkers and wheelchairs.

It was Sunday afternoon, and thank god the kids I coached had no practice and no game. I'd been screaming at them a lot lately. Plant your back foot! Stick up your elbow! Follow through on the ball! Don't stand flat-footed! This isn't fucking Little League! Even I was tired of hearing me scream. They were just sixteen- and seventeen-year-old guys who wanted to be playing some stupid video game or splashing around in the pool or smoking weed in the back seat of a car, and some washed-up, third-rate ballplayer was skinning their asses.

"An eight and one record?" Bimbi said. "I bet no one else in this joint has a grandson whose team has an eight and one record." She made it sound like it was impressive that coaching high school was the only job I could land.

"There was a scout at the last game," I said. A middle-aged man in the bleachers who was no one's dad. "They've got a couple kids on their radar."

Bimbi made a sharp turn toward the activity center. "That's all well and good, Jason, but maybe you should show them what *you* can do with a long ball."

My professional baseball career had ended in a coke-fueled disgrace eight years earlier, but Bimbi still grasped onto the insane hope that some team would suddenly want me to suit up and take third.

Anasazi Meadows was pretty compact, so our weekly tours retraced a lot of the same real estate. When I used to visit Bimbi at Sepulveda Terrace in California, she'd drive us through the nine-hole golf course and show me green-necked ducks in the pond. We'd stop by her friends' apartments for lemon cake and Arnold Palmers. At Anasazi Meadows there was no one to visit, hardly anything to see, just us doing circles through the arid air. But it was better than last winter, when Bimbi just sat in her La-Z-Boy wrapped in some crappy quilt, watching the 24-hour news. That was the worst part about moving her to Santa Fe after Pop died last year. I was her last living family member—and vice-versa—but the cold weather made her poor old joints ache.

"Are you still dating that skinny girl?" Bimbi asked.

"Basically." We'd only been seeing each for one month, and Toni was too young—twenty-two to my thirty-two—and it was too soon after Pilar dumped me for anything serious.

"She's a bad influence."

"What am I, fourteen?"

"You always smell like reefer when you come from her place," Bimbi said.

"What are you talking about? I do not." I hadn't seen Toni yet that day, but was still relieved sunglasses hid my pupils. My last stint in rehab was eighteen months ago, and Bimbi and I had a deal: if I started using again, off to rehab I'd go. "And besides, how would you know what reefer smells like?"

"I lived through the sixties, you know." Bimbi ran a stop sign just as a bent-over woman stepped off the sidewalk. The woman teetered back. "Sorry, Teresa!" Bimbi yelled. Then she said to me, "Maybe the skinny girl's after your money."

"That's pretty unlikely." I didn't have that kind of dough—unlike most trust-fund babies in Santa Fe. My recent inheritance had trickled down from a man who spent his entire life selling refrigerators and stoves in San Bernardino, hoping his son would make it in the bigs one day. Of course, there would have been more money if Pop hadn't paid off my debts and footed the bill for two tours through the Santa Fe Recovery Center. "Relapse is a part of recovery," my counselors used to say. Like that was reassuring.

Bimbi brought the golf cart to a stop at the Anasazi Meadows sign: *Retirement Living for Today and Tomorrow*. One left turn out of there and we'd be on Pasco de Peralta, and a mile or so later heading south on I-25. "What do you say, Bambino?" She smiled crinkled coral lips. "You and me on a beach in Mexico?"

The sun was dropping, making piñon trees dissolve behind lazy orange clouds. Beyond the saffron horizon I saw myself covered in sand, with tequila and salt water licking my limbs. I nodded toward Paseo. "Go for it."

Toni was one of those girls who came from back East to go to college at St. John's, but got exasperated with all the Kierkegaard and Homer and Virgil ("It's all so *abstract*," she said). She ended up working in Kuane's Gourmet Market, instead. We'd met on the Plaza when she was handing out Monopoly money as part of a performance art piece she'd concocted with friends. She gave me a Chance card that said "Advance to St. Charles Place." I figured that was flirting in Monopoly vernacular, and asked for her number.

At first, I worried that our age difference meant Toni was too young for me but, lately, I was starting to wonder if it was more like I was too old for her. A rehab counselor once said my emotional growth was stunted at about nineteen. But I wasn't feeling so nineteen. My brain didn't work in overdrive like this when I was nineteen— and it wasn't working in a good way, like on a cure for AIDS or how to stop global warming or even to remember to buy coffee filters so I'd stop using paper towels and end up swallowing wet grinds at the bottom of my mug every day. Lately, my brain was a tangled mishmash of stats like bases-on-balls and RBI that floated among coconuts and coke-caked mirrors. It all seemed to be gaining momentum as I became more inert. That's why Pilar broke up with me three months ago. "You've become so dreary," she said. Dreary. Who talks that way?

The problem wasn't just whether I was too old for Toni, too *dreary* for her. I knew soon she would press for how my parents died. Whenever people heard that my mother O.D.'d when I was five, they shook their heads with judgment and pity. The few times I told anyone about Pop suffering a cerebral hemorrhage from a falling coconut, they laughed and said, "You're kidding!" Like, for his next bit, my father would plunge off a cliff with an anvil tied around his neck.

Toni lived in a detached studio perched between two towering ponderosas on Jasmine's property. She didn't even pay rent—she just had to take care of Jasmine's garden and shop for her from time to time. Jasmine was one of those "take in stray" types. She also housed a guy named Manny who cooked for her. Jasmine's house is where I went after I dropped off Bimbi in the dining room at Anasazi Meadows. Jasmine's house was a one-story faux-dobe planted on five acres of sagebrush and cottonwood and ocotillo, ruled by her three mangy dogs. The house always smelled like curry, even if Jasmine was only eating peanut butter and honey.

"Hey, man!" Manny was the first to greet me when I walked in, flanked by the mangy mutts. He was stirring a pot on the old gas stove Jasmine salvaged off of Venice Beach in the sixties. When Manny wasn't cooking for Jasmine, he made depressing documentaries that he entered in regional film festivals. One was about a transvestite named Juanita who didn't fit in with Santa Fe's art-queen community, and didn't fit in with the Hispanics, either. He/she/whatever wanted to move to San Francisco or L.A., but didn't have the dough, so was stuck in some trailer park in Española with a Chow Chow named Glinda. I thought about her a lot, how she was probably going to die in that trailer with Glinda licking off her purple eye shadow.

"Dinner smells great," I said. "What is it?"

"Roasted lamb with rosemary," Manny said.

It smelled like curry.

Toni stood in front of the open refrigerator. The cold light bounced around the soft edges of her hips. The guys I coached said Toni had a juicy booty, but said it like *joo-SEH boo-TAY*.

"Hey, you." She reached up on her toes to give me a kiss and a beer. "How's your grandmother?"

"Deadly," I said. "We almost killed an old lady at a crosswalk."

"I wish my grandmother was like that," Toni said. "Mine is this judgmental, lips-pursed kind of person. I call her *Grandmother*."

Jasmine was on the couch watching the Astros and Dodgers and smoking a thinly rolled joint. Jasmine was often smoking a thinly rolled joint that she magically produced from the pocket of her skirt. "Toni told me you played in the majors?" she said.

"No." I sat down next to her on the dog hair-covered couch. She handed me the joint, and I took a toke. "Just Triple-A, a long time ago in Tucson."

"Really?" Manny said from the kitchen. "What position?"

"Third base." I had that kind of arm, the kind that could rocket a ball across my body and to first base before the runner crossed the bag. A season-high batting average of .286 in the minors, but no patience at the plate. I swung at everything. Never let a ball go by. When I hit, I hit hard and into the gap. Sometimes into the stands. But in those clutch situations I couldn't get it done. I'd be up with bases loaded, two outs and an 0-2 count. I should've let a few bad ones go by, because the pitcher was tired and losing his control. I should've fouled a few off. But instead I always took going-for-the-fences swings. I just never wanted to be one of those guys who stood looking as a fastball blew by.

"So, what happened?" Manny asked.

Whenever people asked—which they inevitably did—how I went from being a Triple-A hot prospect to a high school coach, I usually brushed it off with "injury." And it wasn't entirely untrue. If addiction is a disease, then perhaps a gram-a-day habit wasn't that different from a ruptured Achilles tendon.

But two weeks earlier I'd spilled the real story to Toni when we were hammered on tequila shots at The Cowgirl. "Okay, first," I had said, leaning so far toward Toni that my chest was flat against the bar. Red and yellow and green Mexican party flags hung above our heads. "I was doing alotta drugs. Mostly coke." Which seemed especially stupid, since it wasn't the eighties, or something. "Second, I was sleeping with the pitching coach's wife." Which was also stupid, but I didn't see why I should be more loyal to my coach than she was to her husband. "Then, I got suspended for two weeks for not showing up at practice or a game, or something. Then, the coach's wife broke it off with me. And one night when the team was playing, I broke into their house and I stole one of her shoes."

It wasn't even a sexy shoe—it was a navy blue sneaker. I was released mid-season and dove head-first into a coke and whiskey rampage.

The morning after telling this story to Toni, I woke up beside her with a headache that pounded into my toes. "Um, maybe you shouldn't tell anyone what I told you last night," I said. "It wasn't exactly my shining moment."

"Of course," she had said. "What happens in Triple-A stays in Triple-A."

So, Toni looked pretty surprised when we were hanging out with the Astros and Dodgers playing in the background, and I admitted to Manny and Jasmine, "I fucked up." But Toni didn't look surprised like you could knock her over with a feather. She looked how a parent does when they notice their kid tying their shoes for the first time.

"I did some stupid shit and I fucked up my entire career," I said. "I got released and no one would ever sign me again."

Or maybe they would have, but I never tried. I just got in my car with an eight-ball in my pocket and a gram up my nose and drove east out of Tucson. Then north. I was heading to Montana—God, I don't even remember why; I think I actually considered being a *cowboy*—but my car broke down outside Glorieta, and I got towed into Santa Fe.

Jasmine handed me the joint. It was almost down to a roach. "Fucking up is life," she said. "Now let's eat."

I could've told them about the coke—and other sundry substances—and they wouldn't have cared. They weren't invested enough in me, not like Bimbi, not like Pop. But if they knew, they might have felt weird smoking and drinking around me. They might have stopped passing me joints. Or, maybe, they wouldn't have.

Toni and I had dragged her futon and a blanket onto the rigid ground outside her studio. We didn't worry much about being quiet on the futon, partly because we were high and horny from the joint Jasmine produced after dinner, and partly because being quiet didn't seem important among sagebrush and coyotes.

Afterwards, we stared up at the sky. In San Bernardino, the useless glow of headlights and strip malls turned the stars into measly pinpricks. I never really saw stars until I'd been in Santa Fe one week and ran outside in the middle of the night with a bloody nose and fell onto the deer grass. Some of those stars were big and bright, like they wanted to sear into your retinas, and some were barely flickering.

They were all fighting for a place where they could burn themselves into oblivion. Some of them already had—some of those stars were already gone.

Toni said, "I met Pilar today."

"What?" The stars started spiraling around, like they were all being sucked into a black hole.

"She came into the store. She paid with a credit card, and her name was right there." *Pilar Rodriguez.*

I wanted to ask what she bought, like I'd intuit one thing if she bought white truffle oil, and glean another if her basket was loaded with fancy French cheese.

"I told her I knew you," Toni said. "That we're friends."

Friends. I wondered why Toni said that. She could have told Pilar we were dating. Not that Pilar couldn't read between the lines anyway. But still, Toni only said "friends" for a reason. Something to do with me.

"She asked how you are," Toni said.

"What did you say?"

"I said that you're fine." Toni turned to face me. Her blond hair dropped over her shoulder, covering her small breasts. "And it sounded weird even when I was saying it, because it's the kind of thing you say when you don't really mean it. And I did mean it. I don't think you're doing great, and I don't think you're doing bad, either. Anyway. She said that you hadn't been the same since your dad died."

I'd been too dreary.

"And I said, Thank God. People are supposed to be different after someone they love dies. You'd be a pretty messed up guy if you weren't. And then I had to ring up the next person."

I kept my eyes on the mess of stars, but put my arm around Toni. The skin of her cheek was smooth against my chest. It was all smooth against my side, her breasts, her belly, her thighs. I felt so hulking, so hairy.

"Last summer my dad went to Hawaii with some buddies," I said. "He'd been saving for the trip for forever." I pressed my free arm against my forehead, trying to smash it down. "They were playing golf on Kaua'i, and a coconut fell off a tree and hit him on the head."

Beware of Falling Coconuts, a nearby sign said. That's how the golf course protected itself from liability.

"On the head?" Toni sat up, the blanket falling away. "From how high?"

"Pretty high." Those palms had towered over the links for a long time. Gave that coconut enough velocity to fracture Pop's skull, to cause his brain to bleed.

"My God, that's terrible."

"You don't think it's, you know, funny?"

"Only in an abstract way," Toni said. Toni hated the abstract.

"I'd been clean for three-and-a-half years when it happened," I said. "No coke, no pot, no booze, no pills." And I was okay, really, for the first few months. Because the first few months were about the funeral and the appliance store and moving Bimbi. Then entropy stopped, and everything contracted back the other way, towards the tequila. Towards the weed. "I think I'm on a slippery slope."

Toni's face hovered over me, blocking my view of the sky. I closed my eyes, but could still see the stars. Pinpricks burning into my retinas. Some of them already gone. Then there was nothing but smooth skin against my quads, my abs, my pecs. Toni's lips slid in the path of a tear, and landed near my ear. "Fucking coconuts," she whispered.

Bimbi left a note on her door, scrawled on notepaper advertising blood pressure pills. She wrote in the formal cursive that only fourth grade teachers and old women use.

Bambino, meet me at the beauty parlor, 1st floor.

My gray T-shirt was stained with sweat. I'd meant to go home and change, but I ran practice late. I made the guys who swung at everything—guys like I used to be—stand at the plate and only take a cut at every fifth pitch, even if a ball was straight down the center. Anyone who swung—even if they made contact—had to run the bases ten times. A half hour later I was wondering if that was really the best way to teach patience at the plate.

Bimbi sat in the chair with a black plastic cape around her shoulders. The hair dresser was shooting a fog of hairspray over fresh gray curls. "Don't I look like a movie star?" Bimbi asked.

"A total Carol Lombard," I said. Bimbi wasn't one of those old women who was shockingly beautiful in her younger years, where you looked at a sepia photo and sighed, "Wow, you must've had to beat them off with a stick." She was more the sort that people called a "formidable woman."

The hairdresser unsnapped Bimbi's cape, and I gave her a hand while she stepped out of the chair. "Why are you all gussied up?"

"You're taking me to dinner," Bimbi said. Sometimes we ate at the Denny's on Cerrillos. Bimbi always ordered a steak, and I'd say, "Come on, let me take you downtown for a real steak," and she'd say, "You're not spending your dad's hard-earned money so a bunch of brats can treat us like yesterday's garbage."

Bimbi held onto my arm like I was escorting her to a debutante hall. "You're very sweaty," she said.

"I didn't realize I was going on a date. We can swing by my place so I can change."

"It's okay," Bimbi said. "A man should smell a little sweaty. It means you've been working."

It took forever to walk down the hall and out to my car. I tried to be zen about it, tried to just appreciate being in the moment with my Bimbi, noticing the clouds and sky starting to turn orange and pink. More than anything, I didn't want to be annoyed. She couldn't help it, and since she'd been forgiving of a lot of bad behavior that I probably could have helped, it seemed the least I could do was show some patience. But Jesus, she was slow.

"I want enchiladas," Bimbi said when we finally got settled in my car. "Good ones, from that place you're always talking about."

"They're kind of spicy," I said.

"The spicier the better." She switched on the radio. Bob Dylan was singing "Tangled Up in Blue." Bimbi hummed along and looked out the window, like the harmonica had dropped her into some haze of nostalgia.

At the restaurant, Bimbi ordered green chile enchiladas. "And bring me a margarita," she told the waiter. "Use the good stuff." She was still humming Bob Dylan, even though the restaurant speakers piped in U2.

"Bimbi, what's going on?"

"What do you mean?"

"Getting your hair done and wanting enchiladas and margaritas?" I left out the part about Bob Dylan, because I couldn't explain why it was unnerving to hear Bimbi hum that long song.

"I wanted to do something different," she said. "You don't want to do the same thing every day for the rest of your life, do you?"

For the most part, my life was the same every day: wake up, work out, coach the guys, go home. On special days there was dinner at Jasmine's, or movies with Manny, or waking up on Toni's futon. I wouldn't have minded if those weren't special occasions anymore. I wouldn't have minded the chance to get bored with it all.

The waiter set down our drinks. Bimbi used both hands to lift the glass to her crinkled lips. Salt granules stuck in the corners of her mouth. "Now, that's a drink! Your grandfather used to make a helluva margarita. He'd put on a sombrero and cha-cha-cha around the living room."

Pop did that when I was a kid, too. On Taco Tuesdays, he'd lay out ground beef and shredded cheese and shells on the kitchen counter, then he'd put on an enormous sombrero and dance to Tito Puente.

Bimbi eyed me over the rim of her glass. "You shouldn't be drinking," she said.

"It's just one drink."

"That's like being sort of pregnant."

"It's okay, Bimbi," I said, "I'm okay," but my voice sounded wistful.

She stirred the cubes in her glass with a green straw. "This skinny girl . . . those people she lives with," Bimbi said. "They know how to get drugs, don't they? Pills?"

"Sure," I said. "Uppers, downers, pink hearts, white crosses, bennies, OC-40, ludes . . ."

"You're being a smart ass."

"They're good folks who've been incredibly nice to me."

"That's good." Bimbi sipped more margarita. "I don't want you to be alone."

"I'm not alone," I said. "I have you."

"Bambino . . ." She reached across the table and placed a wrinkled hand over mine.

It's like I was suddenly dropped into some made-for-TV movie with weeping violins and long, doleful looks. I couldn't get my gaze out of the salsa. "Shit, Bimbi. What is it?"

"Cancer," she said. "My liver."

The waiter set plates in front of us. The spicy steam of Bimbi's enchiladas whirled toward my tamales. I tilted my empty glass toward the waiter. "I'll have another."

Bimbi moved a chunk of enchilada to her lips, a long strand of cheese still tethered to her plate. She sucked it up, splattering green chile on her cheek.

"How long?" I asked.

"Six months. Maybe less."

"What about chemo?"

"It'll make me sick and weak," she said.

"But if you don't treat it—"

"It'll make me sick and weak." She shook her head. "And the pain . . ."

I reached over with a napkin and dabbed at the green chile on Bimbi's cheek, I kept wiping, even after the chile was gone, tracing the contours of her face with the red cloth. I followed the crescents that made parentheses around her mouth, grazed her blush-stained cheeks, smoothed out the deep crow's feet around her eyes. She tried to smile crinkled lips, no longer coral. All her lipstick had worn off on the rim of her glass.

"So, those friends of yours," Bimbi said. "The ones Toni lives with. They can get lots of pills. Right?"

"Right." I lay my napkin back in my lap.

"Then I think I should meet them."

Jasmine's dining room table was covered with a white linen tablecloth edged with lace. We ate off bone china painted with faded plums, and drank from glasses beveled like a chandelier. Our utensils were Bimbi's wedding silver, which Toni and Jasmine had spent the afternoon polishing. Bimbi sat at the head of the table wearing a lime green pantsuit. "That's what you're wearing?" I'd asked when I picked her up at Anasazi Meadows. "It's festive," she'd said.

At Bimbi's request, Manny prepared Steak Diane. We had shrimp cocktails and gin martinis and played Frank Sinatra in the background. Manny flambéed the steak tableside. I sat transfixed by the flames, as the alcohol evaporated, leaving behind the smell of pepper, garlic, and figs.

"Jason, did you see Manny's tattoo?" Bimbi pointed to Manny's bicep adorned with a Hindu something-or-another. "My son had a tattoo," she told the others. "He got it when he was in Vietnam. A hoochie-koochie girl with perky breasts."

"Your son was in 'Nam?" Jasmine asked.

"I couldn't find that damn place on a map before he went," Bimbi said. "And I drank like a fish the whole time he was gone. The day he came home, I was so happy to see him that I knocked him clean over on the front lawn." She looked out the window like she expected Pop to come ambling up Jasmine's dusty driveway. "It sure is a thing," she said. "Your son being gone."

There was probably something significant I should say, but I didn't want to be too, you know . . . dreary. It's not even as if topics were flooding my head, but before I spit them out my brain deemed them too sad or too trite. It was a vacuum in there. The others seemed so adept, asking questions and telling stories and laughing like it was any old dinner party. I felt trapped in one of my dreams, the ones with baseball stats and coconuts and dusted mirrors.

"Who's ready for dessert?" Toni clapped her hands.

"Oh, I'm much too full," Bimbi said. "But there is something I want." She placed her hand on my forearm, and it startled me, having her touch me. "I want to see you hit baseballs."

"I tossed all my training tapes in the garbage years ago," I said. In between visits to rehab.

"One of you . . ." She swept her hand from one side of the table to the other. "You could pitch to him."

"You've got all that gear in your trunk," Toni said. "All those balls and bats."

That's when you know you've reached a relationship milestone— when a woman's catalogued all the crap you carry in your trunk.

"Let's do it, man," Manny said. "I've never played with a pro."

"Listen, I'm not really—" I said, but everyone was already out of their chairs, heading outside. Everyone except me and Bimbi. I traced my finger around the plums on my plate. "This is really what you want?"

"It's really what I want," she said.

We stood in a clearing of sagebrush and bumpy brown dirt. Manny and Jasmine, and even Bimbi, stood in the outfield, like they trusted that's the only place my balls would go. Toni stood about forty feet away from me with the bucket of balls. "Ready?" she said.

I picked up a maple bat, solid and heavy throughout. It wasn't light in the handle and bulbous at the end like those crap-ass aluminum bats when I was in high school. Now kids were using lumber like the pros. Some big brain must have figured out it would help prepare them for the realities of that world.

Toni took a softball fast-pitch stance. I put my weight on my back foot, my elbow high, my eye on the ball. Toni's pitch wobbled low and inside, and I watched it go by. She picked up another ball from the bucket, and threw again. This time it went wide. Toni's third pitch crossed the plate, right down the middle. It plunked to the ground behind me.

"Swing, damnit!" Manny yelled.

"What are you waiting for, Bambino?" Bimbi called.

"Screw walks!" Jasmine said. "We want home runs!"

They all chanted "Hey, batter-batter, *swing*," like that was going to help me somehow—and in a way, it did, because they weren't taunting me. They were telling me to let it rip.

The next ball was up in the zone, so I swung. The vibration was thick and hard and crackled into the bones of my hands. The ball dribbled up the first base line. One of the dogs ran after it and returned it to Toni. She wiped the slobber off on her jeans.

My hands tingled. "Another," I said.

Toni threw a pitch so low it nearly grazed the dirt, but I golfed it right back to her. It sent a bolt of heat up my arms. I'd hit a million baseballs, but none felt so heavy, so hard.

I gripped the bat tighter. "Another."

On the next pitch I connected with the sweet spot. That sound— the crack of the bat when you know you've hit a long ball—it's not like it sounds in the stands, on the radio, on TV. When you're holding the bat, that crack isn't just in the air or in your ears. It's in your muscles, your tendons, your blood and your bones.

Manny tried to track it down, but he lost it in the sun and the ball landed well behind him.

"That's my Bambino!" Bimbi yelled

My fingers and wrists and arms pulsed from grasping the bat and locking my elbows. *Relax*, Pop told me when I was a kid. *If you're tense, you can't react fast.* Fast meant strong, and strong meant long. I stepped back and extended the bat over my head, down my back. I wiggled my fingers. I came back into stance and thought, *It's just a game.*

Shit, had I ever said that to the kids I coached?

Toni threw down the pipe and I smacked another ball long, long, long. Jasmine ran after it, her skirt flouncing, and her dogs ran after her. That was two in a row, and I know they—Bimbi—wanted a whole damn derby. *Take each pitch one at a time*, my high school coach used to say. *What you've done before doesn't matter. All that matters is this at-bat.* They used to say that in rehab, too—all that matters is the now—and I thought it was such bullshit. Of *course* all the ways you succeeded and fucked up in the past mattered.

This pitch is the only pitch, I thought, and I thought it again and again and again. My elbows relaxed, my shoulders dropped. Toni threw, and *bam!* In a real game, it might have been foul, but in our game it was a homerun.

It was like batting practice, but better. In BP, you're just hitting easy balls to enthrall fans. The pitcher's taking so much off of it that it's like there's nothing on it at all. In BP, there's no stakes, no reality. But standing there with Toni and Manny and Bimbi waiting for my long balls was nothing but truth.

"Throw harder," I said to Toni. I didn't know if she could, but I knew this would make no sense if she didn't.

She smiled with her eyebrows raised. "I don't know if you can take my heat."

"I can handle your heat, girl," I said. "And then some."

Next thing I knew, a fireball was coming at me. The nerves in my hands prickled and I swung too late. The ball flew by me, raising dust in the dirt.

"That's my stuff, baby," Toni said. "You wanna see some more?"

"Give me all you got." I did an Ichiro-like squat, then stood and hit dirt off each shoe with the end of the bat. I stretched out my left arm like I was pointing my finger at Toni, and with my right arm stretched the bat upright, pointing to the sky. At whatever—whoever —was up there.

I was ready for her pitch this time, ready for her heat, relaxed but focused, strong, and I hit that shit over everyone's head. That's the physics of baseball. The faster they came, the harder I could hit.

Toni kept throwing gas and I keep hitting dingers, one after the other, all over Jasmine's sagebrush and piñon and deer grass and ocotillo, into the evening sky turning orange and purple and pink.

Manny whooped and the dogs barked and Bimbi laughed like I hadn't heard her since Pop died.

"Only one more," Toni said. She held up the last ball from the bucket. She nodded at me, and I nodded back.

Toni's pitch and my swing—none of it was slow-motion like you want those moments to be, like the movies make you think they're supposed to be. But as soon as that ball left the end of the bat, my legs gave out and I was kneeling in the dirt, watching that bomb fly. The others held their hands over their eyes, their necks craning along the ball's arc—in front of them, over them, behind them—until gravity finally pulled it to earth. All four of them hooted and yelled. There was sweat in my eyes, sweat in my mouth, dirt on my knees.

"I'll get it." Bimbi said. She took long, determined strides through the sagebrush towards the ball. The barking dogs ran circles around her while she laughed. Her arms were stretched out wide, helping her keep upright. She looked like a prairie falcon ready to take flight.

I was still fighting for breath, and for once that thin, arid air didn't make my lungs burn. Each sharp inhale expanded inside my chest, and each long exhale let something else go. I stayed on my knees while my breath slowly evened out, no more push and no more pull, and I watched my Bimbi march into the saffron horizon.

covered in red dirt

Kimo and I stretched out long in my bed. I ran my finger over his arm wrapped around my waist. I traced the edges of the blotches on his skin, milky white patches blossoming against brown. "It's what Michael Jackson said he had," Kimo said when Kayla asked him what was up with his skin. I'd hushed her: *That's rude.* But Kimo, he didn't mind. "It's just the way I am." People called him Hapa Kimo. Hapa is what locals call folks who are half Caucasian and half something else. Half haole, half Japanese. Half haole, half Samoan. Kimo's mom was haole, his dad Filipino. "Guess my skin wanted to keep Mom close by," he said.

Kimo came by every Tuesday. It was the day he delivered bottled water to the Lawa'i Valley. I once asked him if he had a woman for every day of the week, for every part of Kaua'i. He laughed. "You're crazy. You think they knockin' down doors to get to Kimo?" I wasn't sure what that said about me, or him. He also taught surf lessons and did handyman work. That's how it is in the islands: you have to work three jobs to get by. I only worked one, giving massages at a hotel spa, because John was paying enough child support for me and Kayla.

"Almost Kayla time," Kimo said. I slid out from under his arm. We were always sure to make the bed back up by the time Kayla was home from school. Most days, my daughter came home covered in the island's red dirt. It was on her ankles or her elbows, sometimes on her knees. When it got into her shorts and shirts, there was no cleaning it out. Kayla used to wear white, when we lived on the mainland. She had white dresses and frilly white tops; little white capri pants and even white sandals. But since we moved to Kaua'i last year there was no point. The island made its mark on everyone and everything.

Kimo and I sat on the porch, not saying much, just listening to the way the trade winds swished the palms, when Kayla came walking up the road in her shorts and T-shirt and flip-flops. *Slippers, Mom,* she always reminded me. *That's what they call them here.*

"Howzit?" she said, plopping her backpack on the porch.

"Hey, little wahine," Kimo said. "You ready to hit some waves?"

"I need a snack," she said and headed inside.

"Little grind!" he called after her. "No want your stomach too full."

I waited until Kayla was in the kitchen, away from us. "I'd like it if you didn't talk slang with her," I said.

"That's how people talk round here, Dorrie," Kimo said, just looking out at the breeze, making me believe it was possible to see a breeze. "You been here long enough to know."

Nine months. At first it didn't take me long to slip into the island ways, the slow talk and the slow walking, slang that seemed easier than saying the real words. But after John left us, my attitude went back the other way.

"How about when she needs to get into college?" I asked. Or how about if we're not forever stuck on this island? Someday we might just get back to the mainland, and kids would tease her.

"She's twelve," Kimo said. "Plenty of time till college."

Kayla came back with a fruit roll-up in one hand, her surfboard tucked under the other arm. "Let's rip," she said. "You coming, Mom?"

"You bet." There was no work that afternoon, no tourists wanting me to rub their muscles with coconut-scented oil. The three of us squeezed in the front seat of Kimo's rusted pick-up and drove down the curving road to Po'ipu.

When John and I moved to Kaua'i we bought a small house in Kalaheo, in a valley away from Po'ipu's tourists and desert landscape. Kalaheo is carved out of jungle, blanketed by bamboo and monkey trees and philodendrons with leaves like giant flat fingers. On Po'ipu's south side, it's just dry red dirt and cactus. It's barren like the surface of Mars, except where a mainland developer came in and planted palm trees and thick-blade grass. Orchids, plumeria, yellow hibiscus. If you went the other direction from our house, you'd be in Waimea canyon, deep walls carved away by the river's erosion. If you want something different on Kaua'i, you don't have to go far. John just went North, to Leilani's house. It's rainier there, but greener, too.

Kimo and Kayla took to their boards, paddling out to waves. I sat on the beach with the tourists lazing in the sun. They bring that fake coconut smell with them, painting them slick and brown. When I was fifteen, sixteen, I'd sit in my backyard coated in baby oil, trying for a Valley Girl tan. I thought the burn would wear off into luscious brown. It never really happened that way, but I kept on burning my flesh anyway.

Kimo paddled ahead of Kayla, sometimes looking back for her. Little waves rolled towards them, and Kimo and Kayla slipped over the tops. Like riding a bucking bronco, but gentle. Sometimes a bigger wave came, but too close to the shore, so they grasped the front of their boards and dove under. "Always better to go under or over a wave than through it," Kimo would say.

John didn't want Kayla surfing, still wouldn't want her surfing if he knew she surfed. "It's too dangerous for a young girl," he said. Kayla had been trying to wear him down since before we moved, since we were on the plane. She kept talking about a girl from Kaua'i who lost her arm in a shark attack. "She started surfing again only one month after the shark bit her arm off," Kayla said. "And she's a professional now." The argument did little to sway John, and who could blame him? But for every surfer who gets mauled in a shark attack there are hundreds of thousands who never do. John would never see it that way. But after he left us for Leilani, I figured how he saw things wasn't the only way.

Kayla and Kimo were so far out that I couldn't hear them, they couldn't see me. Not that they were looking for me. I wondered why Kimo never had any kids of his own. Then again, I didn't know that he didn't. I didn't even know if Kimo had ever been married. Hell, I didn't know what he was doing with me, some uptight, middle-aged haole.

Kimo waved a windmill through the air at Kayla. *Take this one.*
She paddled to catch the lip of the wave. Then she was up on her feet.
Sometimes I imagined her on that board when I did Warrior Two in
yoga. I'd imagine the salty spray around my face, a roar so loud I
couldn't hear. No mirrored walls in front of me, no click-click-click
of the overhead fan, no rubber mat sticking me to the ground.

Her first few seconds upright were a fight between Kayla and the
wave: who would ride who. She gave a good knee bend, and won
that battle. The wave pulled her along, like she was tethered to the
other end.

Whatever tension had been keeping Kayla upright was severed,
and the water tunnel crashed down. I shielded my hands over my
eyes, afternoon sun grimacing. Kimo paddled toward where Kayla
had gone down. Her yellow board popped up, and then her head.
The ocean spit her right back out. Kimo held out his hand and
pulled her on her board. The two paddled back out again. They
went to fight another battle against the sea.

John had Kayla every other weekend, more if he wanted. There was
no official custody agreement. That could have never happened on
the mainland. John would have had one of the partners at his firm
draw up reams of paper. Everything would have been official, from
the separation to the division of assets to the final divorce. But after
we moved to the islands, John lost that drive. Killer instinct, he used
to call it.

Every Friday John drove clockwise around the island to pick up
Kayla from my house. On Sundays, I drove counter-clockwise to
retrieve her. His way was worse, getting choked in Friday rush hour
in Lihu'e. Nothing like L.A., of course. This traffic was just one long
lane going one way, one long lane going another. When I drove up
on Sunday, the worst of the traffic wasn't in Lihu'e, but up North.
Tourists heading for Hanalei beaches and the Na Pali Coast. Pulling
their cars aside to snap pictures of rainbows.

Leilani's house was inland, surrounded by mango trees. "We eat
a lot of mangos when I'm there," Kayla told me. "Like, all the time.
It drives me crazy." I knew she said this just for me. Leilani's three
mangy dogs barked and followed my car up the long driveway to her
house. Wagging tails, ears forward. No teeth bared.

"Are you early?" John was on the porch, wearing a shirt bursting with orange plumeria.

I looked at my watch. "Not really."

"Kay, your mom's here!" John yelled into the house. "Get your stuff together."

"Yeah, coming!" my daughter yelled back.

John stood against the porch railing, looking out at the mangos like I wasn't on the top step, my arms folded across my chest. "You want some tea?" he said. "Or juice? Hey, Leilani!" he called behind him. "What kind of juice do we have?"

"Why you yelling?" Leilani stepped through the front door wearing peach-colored scrubs. I couldn't tell if she was coming from the hospital or going. "Hi, Dorrie."

She wasn't pretty like the word Leilani makes you think, long and thin, on an exotic postcard. But she wasn't some big Samoan either, a formidable force of womanliness. She was an average woman. Except she was more.

"Bring some juice out," John said. "We can sit. Talk story." It— *talk story*—sounded stupid coming out of John's mouth. It's what everyone said around here, Kimo all the time, Kayla and even me, but from John it sounded like trying to force a round peg into a square hole.

"I'm not thirsty," I said.

"Maybe some cookies, then?" John said.

"John, come inside," Leilani said. He followed her in.

All the windows in Leilani's wood house were open to capture whatever breeze made it that far inland. It also pushed out John and Leilani's voices.

"What are you doing, trying to get us to all sit and grind?" she asked.

"There's no reason we can't be friendly," John said.

"You left her for another woman," Leilani said. "She doesn't want to be your friend."

"She'll get over that," John said. "She'll move on."

He didn't know about me and Kimo. I didn't want him to think I'd moved on.

"John, just let her be," Leilani said. "Show her respect."

It made me want to say, "Yeah, I'll have some mango juice," to sit on Leilani's porch and eat coco-mac cookies, just to prove her wrong, because it pissed me off that she was right. But Kayla skipped through the front door, carrying her backpack and duffle bag. "Okay, Mom," she said. "Let's go."

There was hardly any traffic on our side as we drove clockwise again. I'd gotten hungry, standing on that porch, so we stopped at a roadside stand in Anahola for burgers and shakes. We ate at a round picnic table with tourists. Two wild chickens and a rooster wandered around our perimeter, waiting for us to drop a piece of meat. The island was overrun with feral roosters, crowing day and night. We watched the birds scratch and scrape, waiting for their prey.

Next Tuesday, when we were still lying in bed, Kimo said, "Let's you and me get some dinner on Saturday. While Kayla's with her dad."

"Why?" I asked. Kimo and I had never been outside of the house together, not unless we were at the beach with Kayla, getting shave ice, eating Puka Dogs.

Kimo pulled himself on top of me and kissed my lips. "If you're this pretty in the daylight, you must be a goddess at night."

There wasn't much more to say, really.

We ate at a Chinese barbeque joint in Lihu'e, but didn't eat barbeque. There were too many places to get island barbeque, so we shared shrimp with choi sum and sizzling scallops with black bean sauce. Fried coconut ice cream for dessert. The place was full of brown-skinned locals, a few haole, like me, and some tourists brave enough to go off the beaten path. I kept thinking that most of those locals were technically hapa, but none of them looked hapa like Kimo. His brown and white skin, the way he didn't care much about it, made him seem royal. Maybe Kimo was right, maybe there was something about seeing each other in nightlight that made us divine.

We went back to Kimo's place, a house he shared with two other guys. One was tending bar, the other waiting tables. The living room furniture was worn wicker, dusty walls covered by tapestries of whales and sea turtles. The air smelled like old apple cider vinegar.

"It's how locals live," Kimo said, even though I'd said nothing. I got the feeling that he could read my thoughts. That maybe he had some sort of island mojo.

His bedroom was small, but immaculate. No clothes on the floor, no clutter on his nightstand. The bed made with crisp-looking sheets. His mattress sat on a bed frame of carved koa wood.

"It was my tutu's," he said, as I ran my hand over the reddish-brown wood. "She gave it to my dad, and my dad gave it to me."

My grandmother gave me a brooch, once. It was gold-plated, shaped like a snowflake, mindlessly picked out of her jewelry box. *Here*, she'd said, *you can have this*. I lost it in the backseat of some guy's car years ago.

Kimo's bed was bigger than a back seat. We stretched out and up, laid flat and round. We bathed in the scent of plumeria and sex. We were royalty.

Next Tuesday I worked at the spa. Another massage therapist called in sick and I had to cover her shift. I don't know if anyone really got sick—more likely someone was heading to big waves on the North Shore. "Cough, cough," they'd spew into the phone. "I have a sore throat." It meant I wouldn't see Kimo, but he was going to drop by the house and pick up Kayla for surfing anyway.

I gave massages to three couples that day, folks who just got married or wanted to pretend like they just did. Olina and I worked together, standing side by side in a thatched hale. Her hands glided over one client, mine over the other. We worked separate, but moved together. The rain beat outside.

Olina and I were standing outside the hale, waiting for the couple to put on their long terry robes. Rain smacked the tops of broad leaf plants, then slid into the garden. There was water from the waterfalls, water from the sky. When it rained like this, it was easy to believe the island would just return to the ocean.

"So, I hear you were out with Hapa Kimo the other night," Olina said.

"Where did you hear that?"

She waved a hand. "Oh, you know how people talk. Nothin' better to do."

"We had scallops," I said.

"Just scallops, yeah?" she poked me in the ribs. If Olina knew that Kimo and I had Chinese BBQ in Lihu'e, then could the news travel to John? Sure, it was an island of fifty-thousand people, but only fifty miles of road between us. Maybe there was some math, some physics, some law that made information travel faster. Then John would think it was okay, dragging me and Kayla all the way across the ocean, only to leave us amid giant leaves for mango trees.

"Hey, Dorrie?" It was the receptionist who stood behind the spa's front desk looking impossibly pretty. "Phone call for you. Says it's an emergency. About your daughter."

All the smells and sounds of the island shut down. I could have been on the surface of Mars, airless and ice cold.

Kayla was at Mahelona Memorial Hospital in Kapaʻa. She got hit by a big wave, and then another, and she couldn't get to her board. The waves kept coming, and one finally threw her into the rocks. Ancient lava, black and jagged, tearing into my baby girl's skull. She was bleeding in the brain, needed surgery to stop it. I signed the papers, called John. Waited for him to show.

I sat next to Kimo in the waiting room. His hair was still wet. "Why is she here?" I asked.

He put his hand on top of mine, but I refused to give him a hand. Just a fist, so his hand was more like a piece of paper in rock, paper, scissors. "I know. It's hard to understand."

"No," I said, pulling my fist away from him. "Why the fuck is she *here*? On this part of the island? Why were you surfing up North?"

"She wanted to surf where Bethany surfed," he said.

"You mean where Bethany got her arm bitten off by a shark?"

"That's not what happened," Kimo said gently.

"I know what happened." I stood. "You took my daughter someplace dangerous. You let her do something that could kill her."

"Dorrie . . ." Kimo reached up, pulled my hand. "She's going to be fine. She'll be fine."

Kimo didn't know if Kayla would be fine. I didn't know it, John didn't know it, and Leilani didn't know it either. Even if Kayla was fine, John would be pissed. Pissed enough to take Kayla away from me.

Leilani walked around the corner, just wearing shorts and a T-shirt, like it was any old day. "John's on his way," she said. "Had his phone turned off. Just got the message."

"Have you checked on Kayla yet?" I asked. "How is she?"

"The surgery's coming along," Leilani said. "Right now she's okay." Then Leilani looked at Kimo. "You had that looked at yet?"

"No time," Kimo said and touched his head. I didn't see them before, the scrapes and scratches on his forehead and his arm. Red bleeding into the borders of his brown and white.

She said something in Tagalog, and he said something back that I couldn't understand. She peeked closely at his skull.

Kimo put Kayla in the ocean, and Kimo pulled her out. But it didn't feel like a zero-sum game. Especially since I knew John could turn back to his killer-instinct ways. If he took Kayla away, I'd have no reason to stay. But I still wouldn't go back to the mainland, where plants were small and turned brown and dry. I'd stay here, alone, just for those two weekends a month when I could drive counter-clockwise for my daughter. I'd be stuck with half of me on one side of the island, half of me on the other.

The elevator bell dinged down the hall. I waited for a doctor or a nurse to deliver the news. I waited for a priest to take my hands. I waited for John to be harried and irate. I waited for John to punch out Kimo. I waited for John to take Kayla away. I waited to be expelled from this uncertain paradise. I waited for my daughter, dressed in bright white.

astronomical objects

My lover's fingers are long. When he stretches them out, they bow in the middle. When they bend, he can span five frets. He sits on the wide window sill, the guitar resting on his bare legs. The blond wood so much lighter than the hair on his arms, his chest, his thighs.

The room is warm. He turned up the heat as soon as we walked in. That way we could toss aside the sheets and the blankets and duvet of which the hotel is so proud. Their bed is a heavenly body, but for us, it has no wings. Those heavy sheets and blankets and duvet would keep us tamped flat. We sit and we stand and we twist and we bend. In a chair, over a table, on the floor. The bed is a prop, a place to find balance, but we rarely lie flat.

I sit on the floor below my lover on the wide window sill. My hand wraps around his ankle, but my thumb and fingers cannot touch. His guitar notes slide down.

"It's almost four-thirty," he says.

I let go of his ankle. "I have to go."

My plane takes off late. He was in the shower when I left. This is how we say goodbye. Kissing at the curbside is how others go. We do it with him naked and me dressed. Steam fills the bathroom. When I step into the hotel hallway, my lover is tucked away deep. There is snow on the ground.

I arrive home after midnight. The bedroom is cool and dark. A black cat purrs on my pillow. I undress and slide underneath the quilt.

"When did you get home?" My husband's voice, cloudy with sleep.

"Just now."

He turns on his side and puts his arm around my waist. His hand rests on my belly. I fall back into his curve.

I am paid to pry. I ask the questions their lovers will not. Their wives, their children, their moms. I ask about the drugs and the sex and who inspired that song. What did you want to be when you were six, or twelve, or last week? Did your father hit you or your mother love you, and what about that groupie who looks underage? And what about your death, what do you think that will be like? I'm not going to die, they say. Or, I'll probably die next week.

I interview them in Los Angeles and New York and Atlanta. Philadelphia and Boston. Seattle. My lover is a troubadour. Sometimes he's in these towns. Sometimes he's not.

My lover's hips are sturdy and strong. I squeeze them tight with my thighs. We're on the couch, because the chair has arms. It has casters, too.

"We'll roll," I had said.

"Sounds fun," he said. "Let's try." He sat bare in the chair. Tried to keep it still by holding onto the wall.

I shook my head. "My legs won't fit."

He dropped his arms over the sides. "Like this."

"Then I won't be able to move," I said.

"Well, we can't have that." He went to the couch. He sat, legs together, and I slid on.

The couch is against a window. Over his shoulder, through the glass, is a rooftop garden. A wrought iron bench, potted plants. All the flowers in bloom.

"Jesus," he says. "Sweet Jesus." He doesn't even believe in God.

Later, he reads to me out loud. An article about the Kuiper Belt. Astronomical objects, far away. Cold.

She's an attorney, tall and tan, smart and kind. My husband married her the day after college graduation. They were sweethearts in high school. Lovers in college. Divorced by thirty.

"I'm friends with my ex-wife," my husband said on our third date. "That's fine," I said. I'd dated men who weren't friends with their exes. They were full of hate.

She came to our wedding, wore a dress that shimmered gold. She brought a date—I don't remember his name. She and I danced together. The foxtrot, I think.

Two years ago she told us she'd met a musician. "Maybe you've heard of him," she said.

I had. He was that kind of guy.

"You should interview him," she said, and I would.

Fifteen-hundred words and a picture. His guitar in his lap. Fingers spanning across five frets.

They're in town for the weekend. He plays one show tomorrow night, but the rest of their time is for my husband and me.

We cook on the grill, eat on the patio. The summer corn is sweet. Butter drips onto his chin, and she wipes it away. My husband's hand rests on my thigh. We talk about work, about where he's playing next. My lover says Phoenix and Austin and L.A.

"You'll be in L.A., too, won't you?" my husband asks.

"Really?" my lover says. "Then we should have dinner."

My husband's hand is heavy. Hot.

I usually pry in living rooms, or recording studios, or hotels. But with him, it was near the pit of a fire. We arranged for the interview by e-mail, and I flew to their town. She was having a party at her house, on the beach. He suggested I come by.

She had hugged me hello. Too bad my husband couldn't come, too.

"It's just work," I said. "I'm here today, gone tomorrow."

We cooked fish over a fire, corn in the coals. We drank Long Island Iced Tea. "Come on," he said. "Let's do this thing."

We sat in the sand. My tape recorder rolled. I asked the questions no one else would. And then he asked them back. We stood over the fire and warmed our hands. We talked about camping, in the mountains, as kids. His fingers were hot in my hair.

"Ash," he said. He held the gray flake between us. It dissolved in his fingers. Back inside, I hugged her goodbye. His eyes had more questions from across the room.

The next morning I e-mailed him from my hotel. Thank you for the interview, I said. It should be out in six weeks. And by the way, my hair has that smell of toasting marshmallows and cold mountain air and stars sprinkled like wildflowers in the sky. It was a good interview, he wrote back. I'm looking forward to the article. As for your hair . . . perhaps the less said the better. But I feel like there's more to say.

I was in Denver alone. My lover was at his home, at the beach, with her. I interviewed this band at Red Rocks, in the hills. They smoked a joint while my tape recorder rolled. When I got into my car, there were a thousand stars in the sky. Burning far away, bright.

The black cat purrs at the foot of our bed. I undress and crawl under the sheet. I roll over, try to see my husband in the moonlight. His back is white.

"It's hot in here," I say to the ceiling, but it doesn't respond.

"There's a leaf stuck to your boot," my lover says.

I sit on the edge of the bed. He peels it away from my three-inch heel. It's large and red, from a maple tree. His hand slides up the black leather. Onto skin. Into wet.

"No panties," my lover says. He stands straight, unbuttons his jeans, pushes them to the floor. He pulls off my skirt and grabs my ankles. My back is flat.

The black leather slides and slides and slides. Across his shoulders, slick with sweat.

He sits on the edge of the bed. My chest is pressed against his back, my legs wrapped around his waist. His guitar rests on my ankles. Boots on the floor, unzipped.

He plays three notes. Long, short, long. He says, "They're having an affair."

Long, long, short.

"I know."

He sets down his guitar. On top of my boots. "They write love letters."

Our e-mails are guarded. Short. Everything unsaid. But they don't seem to know what you hold on to. What you never say.

"Is it because—?"

"No," he says. "They did it all on their own."

He stands. My crossed ankles fall away. He walks to the thermostat, turns down the heat. Then he starts at the foot of the bed. He crawls to the top. He makes himself flat.

"Come on," he says.

I am flush with his thighs, his belly, his chest. His arm reaches down. Long fingers grab onto the sheet. He pulls it up, over our heads.

a proportional response

I hate military guys. I have hated military guys ever since their war games caused my friends' plane to be bombed over Lockerbie in 1988. But here Jack and I are, eating Thanksgiving dinner with our new neighbor, Suzanne, and her military ex-husband and their daughter, Mandy. Suzanne's dining room table is covered with an enormous turkey, stuffing, mashed potatoes, Brussels sprouts, maple-glazed sweet potatoes, whiskey gravy, and Parker House rolls. It's more food than any five people on Earth could ever eat.

"I guess I got a little carried away," says Suzanne's ex from the head of the table. His name is Randy and he speaks with an accent suckled on the South.

"Do you say grace?" I ask. I never say grace but love the sound of the phrase. Like thanking an unknown entity for your meal actually bestows a quiet elegance on the table.

"We're not religious," Mandy says. "Well, Dad is a little, but Mom and I are pagans, so we don't pray." She wears a T-shirt with bright green lettering that says: *I Got This Shirt for My Wife (Awesome Trade!)*.

"We've struck a compromise," Randy says, passing the platter of turkey. "While we're eating, we go around the table and say what we're thankful for."

Suzanne says she's grateful Mandy's a smart kid and isn't pregnant or strung out on crack. Mandy says she's psyched to be passing Spanish—which she attributes to watching Mexican soap operas—and she gets to learn about astrology—no, wait, *astronomy*—from Jack.

"And I'm grateful all that stuff in Iraq is winding down," she says, "and that Dad's getting old so maybe he won't get deployed again and could even move somewhere closer by."

During the course of Mandy's many uninvited visits next door, she's told me her dad is a Navy General stationed in Mongolia, and her mother is royalty from Newfoundland, which makes Mandy an Inuit princess. If I had believed, for one second, that Mandy's dad was actually in the Navy, I wouldn't have accepted Suzanne's invitation for Thanksgiving dinner.

"These rolls just melt in your mouth," Jack tells Randy. "Did you bake these, too?"

"No, sir. Those and the pie crusts are store bought."

"They don't teach pastry skills in the Navy, huh?" I say.

"Only in officer training school," Randy says. "But I worked my way up the ranks."

Jack can make delicious ice cream sundaes, and not much else. On our third date he took me on a nighttime picnic with a backpack of pre-cut carrots, Doritos, and ranch dressing. He also brought a telescope and showed me Arcturus and Vega and Saturn's largest moon. That night I decided I didn't need a man who could whip up fabulous risottos.

"Libby, what are you grateful for?" Suzanne asks. "Wow, doesn't that word start sounding lame when you say it as much as we are?"

"Yes," I say. "It does."

Jack nudges my shin under the table.

"Well, I'm grateful that Jack and I are living together." He'd been asking for nearly a year. The last time he asked, there was something different about the light in his bedroom. The walls melted in a warm glow that I assumed was all about us. Our coupleness. It wasn't until we were setting up house together that I realized the yellow light came from the fluorescent light bulbs Jack uses. "And I guess I'm just happy I'm here," I add on.

Of course, I don't really mean *here*, as in at Suzanne's table with her weird daughter and squinty-eyed ex. I mean here, as in alive. For more than a decade after my friends were killed, I couldn't claim that.

"Amen to that," Randy says. "I'm grateful I get to be here with my two girls. And I suppose I've got to echo my daughter, over there. I can't complain about the noise in Iraq dying down."

He makes it sound as if the violence is some annoyance that can be easily rectified by turning a knob to the left. *I can still hear it!* I want to yell.

I pour myself another glass of wine.

We eat pie in Suzanne's living room, and pass another bottle of wine. We wrap our tongues around pumpkin and nutmeg, seeing how far we can stretch small talk before it snaps loose. Randy asks if I always wanted to be a masseuse.

"Massage therapist," I say. "I was actually going to be an actor."

"No shit?" Suzanne folds her long legs underneath her on the couch. "Like, in movies?"

"Plays. But after college I moved to Albuquerque to take care of my dad."

This living room isn't the place to explain that I had wanted somewhere to hide. Someplace where, when people learned I'd gone to Syracuse, they wouldn't immediately ask, *Oh, did you know anyone on that plane?*

Jack stroked the inside of my wrist. The night he'd shown me Saturn's largest moon is when I told him about my friends' bodies raining from the sky over the pastures of Scotland. Since the bombing, I have been with many men, in many different ways. But Jack is the first one I told about what happened to my friends. Which means he is the only one.

"Albuquerque's pretty far from Broadway," Mandy points out. She's sandwiched herself between me and Jack on the couch. "Like a billion miles."

"So Randy," I say. "Mandy told me you're stationed in Mongolia."

"I never said Mongolia," Mandy says. "I don't even know where that is."

"Where did you get Mongolia from?" Suzanne runs her finger through a smear of whipped cream and brings it to her lips. "Isn't it landlocked?"

"Not a lot of need for Naval presence in Mongolia," Randy agrees.

"Not a lot of need for Naval presence in lots of places," I say.

"I guess my bosses think differently," Randy says, "I just go where they tell me."

I never used to think about politics. They were boring and loud and made everyone look ugly. *But the personal is political,* my best friend Tory used to implore from our dorm room floor. *Telling the truth is a revolutionary act.*

Randy's accent has become more languid with the wine. "Let's say you have a massage patient—"

"Client."

"Okay, client, who talks through his entire massage, and he's against everything you're for. He's going on and on about how lazy his wetback gardener is—"

"Randy!" Suzanne hits him in the shoulder and he jerks. Merlot leaps from his glass, onto Jack's thigh.

"I'm so sorry." Randy bolts upright. "It's why they don't put me in charge of missiles."

"It's okay," Jack says. "It's just—"

"Red wine," Suzanne says. "Yikes. I'll get you a sponge. Or do you need hairspray?"

"That's ink." Mandy rolls her eyes. "You need club soda."

"Come on," Suzanne waves Jack across the room. "I think I have some in the basement."

Randy watches them walk away, he seems to be watching Suzanne's long legs.

"So," Randy says. "Would you still give him a massage?"

"Who?" I ask.

"The racist."

"Oh, him. Sure, because that's my job—"

"Exactly."

"But I'd ask him not to say hateful things while on my table." But

I probably really wouldn't. It was the sort of scenario we'd practiced in massage school when learning about "boundaries," and it always seemed clear in that pristine atmosphere. In reality, I'd probably just give him a crappy massage, hoping he'd never call again.

"I can't exactly tell my superior officer, or the President, for that matter, that he shouldn't place troops where he sees fit."

"Actually, I think you can," I say. "The First Amendment says something about that."

"And the Second Amendment says something about the right to bear arms," Randy says. "Wanna show me your weapon?"

"Only if you show me yours."

Randy raises his eyebrows and leans back in the couch. Through the course of the evening, his eyes have become less squinty.

"Mom and Jack sure are taking a long time." Mandy's voice is as fervent as her psychedelic orange lipstick.

Jack and Suzanne's lilting laughter announces their arrival before their footsteps. The front of Jack's khakis have faded from deep red to an embarrassed blush.

"So, have you finished all that icky political talk?" Suzanne asks.

"It seems we've moved on," Randy says.

Suzanne holds up an empty bottle. "Should I open another?"

Jack and I look to each other for a silent conference. His eyes say something about wanting to get back to the John Lennon biography he's reading. Or maybe he wants sex. Either way, we say our goodbyes and thank yous and it was really delicious. Randy shakes my hand. His handshake is military firm, but warm like you'd expect from a man who spent hours in front of the oven and over the stove, cooking a feast for his family and the strangers from next door.

In the bedroom, Mr. Puddlepots lies on my pillow, licking a gray paw. "I think I might have flirted with Randy," I say.

"Really?" Jack pulls his sweater over his head. "I didn't notice."

"You were in the basement with Suzanne." I walk to the bathroom and squeeze toothpaste on my brush.

"Ahhh, the basement, where Suzanne was helping me clean off the thigh of my pants."

I come back into the bedroom with my toothbrush hanging from my mouth. "You don't think . . . do you think they were trying to get us to swing or something?"

Jack unzips his pants. "That guy? No. I think they were drunk and probably want to fuck each other, and we were getting some of the overflow."

I return to the bathroom and spit. "It's amazing," I call back, "that you can sound so practical and so dirty at the same time."

Back to the bedroom, Jack is lying on his side wearing nothing but an erection.

"Here's to overflow," I say. I push Mr. Puddlepots off the bed. He hisses, then meows, then wanders away like it was what he meant to do all along.

I still dream of my dead friends. I dream of them as they were when I last saw them in London: young, fiery, bathed in arrogant wisdom. There were thirty-five Syracuse University students on the plane, and I knew eleven of them well. We'd all been in the fine arts program. Our love is what happens when artistic souls recognize each other. We rushed together like twins separated at birth.

Tory and I shared a flat in London, just like we had in Syracuse. Even though I was three inches taller than Tory, we wore each others' clothes. We wore each others' earrings. She was wearing a pair of mine when the plane went down. They were silver hoops. Nothing special.

People at school always said they couldn't think of one of us without thinking of the other. I was grossly aware of this after the bombing, when I wandered around campus with everyone staring at my phantom limb. It did more than itch. It wept a thick black pus.

Jack is snoring when I wake the morning after Thanksgiving. I slip downstairs to start coffee, feed Mr. Puddlepots, and retrieve the newspaper from the frosted porch. Alongside the paper is a tin of muffins. On top is a note with black block printing: Happy Day After Thanksgiving! From Mandy & Randy.

I examine the muffins for signs of mischief—not that I'm entirely sure how to spot muffin mischief. But with Mandy you can never be too sure. I tear off a top and taste it. It's pumpkin, predictable. Like Randy.

"Hey, babe." Jack's bedhead hair is like the Crab Nebula, with tentacles branching out in a dozen different directions. "Are those muffins?"

"Randy and Mandy left them for us."

Jack sits at the table eating two muffins—tops first, then bottoms.

"I wonder if he was in the Strait of Hormuz," I say. The small waterway in the mid-East became exponentially large in my mind after my friends were killed.

"Who?"

"Randy. He's the right age."

"True," Jack says. "But there's at least a hundred other places he could have been stationed."

"Wherever his bosses tell him to go, right?"

People—the media, the prosecutors, even some of my friends' parents—believe the bomber was hired by Gaddafi to retaliate for America sinking a Libyan ship and for bombing Tripoli in the mid-eighties. The bomber was sentenced to life in prison but got let out this past August. Compassionate leave, they called it. He's supposedly dying.

He still swears he's innocent, even though the suitcase holding the bomb was traced directly to him. He did it—I know he did it, but I don't think he was hired by Gaddafi. More likely he was working for Iran.

The summer before my friends were killed, the U.S. shot down an Iran Air jet over the Strait of Hormuz, two days before the Muslim holiday *eid al-adha*. It was a passenger jet, but the US Navy said they'd mistaken it for a hostile craft. 238 Iranian passengers were killed. Sixteen Iranian crew members. Five months later on the Pan Am jet, 243 American passengers were killed. Sixteen American crew members. It was four days before Christmas.

"Ask him," Jack says. "He seems like a pretty up-front guy."

"What would be the point?" I say. After all, what if Randy had been in the Strait of Hormuz in the Eighties, then what would I say?

Thanks for the muffins and for being involved in the war games that killed my friends? And what if he wasn't anywhere near the Gulf? What if he was in Shanghai? It would be just one more person not taking the blame.

On Saturday Jack takes his seniors on an overnight to an observatory near Pike's Peak. It's their reward for slogging through a semester of physics equations and chemical suffixes. "You're sure you're okay?" he asks me before leaving. He's been gently hovering since I started thinking about the Gulf, the Strait, planes falling from the sky. "I could get someone to cover for me."

"No, go," I say. "I'm fine." I'll go to work, then come home and crawl under the covers, maybe listen to the TV.

Work means being in a dimly lit room with soft music, and my hands connected to another body. That day I give massages to an accountant, and a bride, and a woman whose mother just died. Muscle fibers give me a path to follow. Knots give me something to work out.

I want to take the grief seeping from the woman's pores and sweep it into a corner where it will eventually degrade. But I know that's not how grief works. It makes its way deep inside of you, becoming a part of your blood and fascia.

I massage her grief gently, help guide its way inside.

When I pull into my driveway, Randy's brushing dusty snow off Suzanne's sidewalk. He holds up his hand in a terse wave. Military guys even wave stiffly, lest they look too gay.

I open my trunk and lift out a basket of oil-stained sheets. Randy's instantly at my side. "Here, let me."

"No, I've got it." I'm used to carrying the basket like a toddler perched on one hitched hip. I can open doors, make phone calls, search for my keys.

"Okay, well—"

"Were you in the Strait of Hormuz?" I ask. "In the Eighties?"

Randy doesn't appear surprised by my left-field question. "On a destroyer."

"The *Vincences?*" That was the ship that shot down the Iran Air jet.

"No," Randy says. "Libby, what are we talking about?"

"My friends," I say. "My friends were on the plane blown up over Lockerbie. My best friends."

I was booked to take that flight home with my friends. But I was seeing a guy there, in London, and wanted to say goodbye. We spent my last day in London in bed, most of the time not sleeping, except when it really mattered the most, when I was supposed to be in a cab on the way to Heathrow with Tory.

"Libby, I'm . . ." Randy looks sideways toward the bare branches of cottonwoods. In the few hours I've spent with him, he's never not looked me, or anyone else, in the eyes. "I'm sorry."

I shift the basket to my other arm, my other hip. "Listen, it's cold out here, and I haven't eaten dinner, and I just want to set this down—"

"Of course. I understand."

"Do you want to grab a bite to eat?" I hadn't realized that, after twenty years, there were any more puzzle pieces left, much less one wedged beneath my foot.

I order Kung Pao chicken and Randy goes for sweet and sour fish, and there's no talk of sharing. We both order vodka tonics and don't talk until they arrive. We take long drinks, then set the glasses back on the table. It's like a checkered flag being waved.

"I was twenty-one," Randy says. "Our job was to make sure all countries could navigate the Strait of Hormuz freely. It was called Operation Earnest Will. Do you know much about the Strait of Hormuz?"

"I've seen it on a map." Tory's parents told me to look it up. They said this place was the reason their only daughter was cut down at age twenty. They told me a lot of things, and I never knew what was true and what was their grief looking for someone to blame.

"It's ridiculously narrow," Randy says. "When you're passing through, Iran's right there, super close, and they're not so thrilled about all this coming and going. So they've got guys with guns sitting there all the time. Pointed at you. Everyone's a little tense under even the best of circumstances."

I wonder what "the best of circumstances" looks like in the Persian Gulf. Is there ever a day with rainbows and breezes and ukuleles?

"One day my ship was traveling in convoy," Randy says. "And the frigate ahead of us hit an Iranian mine. It blew through the hull and the keel broke. I mean, the goddamn *keel*. Of a four-hundred-and-fifty-foot ship."

When the bomb exploded on the 747, it tore the plane into four pieces. There was the cockpit and the fuselage and an engine and a wing. Those were the main parts, at least, the big parts that made the one blip on the radar screen turn into four. I've always wondered if radar picked up the smaller objects, the suitcases and seats and bodies plummeting down.

"We all knew there'd be a response," Randy says. "America wasn't going to just sit there with no retaliation."

There always has to be retaliation.

"About three days later we got the order to bomb an Iranian oil platform. We gave the folks working on it the chance to evacuate—"

"How magnanimous," I say.

"We weren't trying to kill anyone," Randy says. "It was supposed to be a *statement*. A proportional one. But they wouldn't leave and started firing on us. Next thing you know, harpoons and bombs and bullets were flying all over the goddamn place."

The waitress deposits our plates in the middle of the table, along with another round of drinks. "It always felt like chaos," Randy says. "Even when it looked calm. At any moment you could get shot, or your ship could hit a mine, or a harpoon could launch at you."

We pile rice onto our plates. We spoon spicy chicken, sweet and sour fish. We drink our drinks.

Randy says, "When that Iranian airliner got shot down, I wasn't surprised."

"Were you surprised about Lockerbie?" That became the shorthand for the tragedy: the name of the town onto which the plane and body parts showered.

"No. Not surprised. I felt . . ." Randy sets down his chopsticks. "Never mind."

"What?"

"It doesn't matter. It's not the point."

"What's the point of any of this?" My words float around, get lost in my spicy peppers, in Randy's sour fish.

"I was relieved," he says. "That the retaliation finally happened. I know that makes me an asshole, but—"

"Randy." He doesn't know what he's saying. Why I want to stop him.

"I don't blame you if you want to kick me in the balls."

"How did you know?" I ask. "That Lockerbie was retaliation for the Iranian plane. I mean, it was floated out there as a theory, but Libya was blamed."

"Listen, I ain't one of those nutcases who believes that the CIA planned 9/11 or Neil Armstrong never really walked on the moon," Randy says. "But I know what a proportional response looks like."

I poke a red chili with my chopstick. Its skin is shriveled, and I want to believe that makes it benign. But I've fallen for that before, thinking, *How bad could it be?* I push it to the side of the plate.

We stop at a park alongside the Highline Canal to look at the stars. "Mandy showed me this place," Randy says. "She said she comes here a lot to think." He points to Fomalhaut, the only star bright enough to outshine light pollution. "She told me it's nicknamed The Lonely One."

I know it's possible the bright light isn't a star at all. It could just be Jupiter, far heavier than all the other planets in the solar system combined, but only a fraction-of-a-fraction as dense as our sun.

"Mandy told me Suzanne's from Newfoundland," I say.

"Fresno."

"And you have a purple heart."

"Actually," Randy looks down from the sky. "That one's true. I was on the *Cole* when it was attacked."

After 1988 there wasn't a single terrorist attack against the United States—on foreign or domestic soil—that I didn't hear about. Tory's mother called whenever this sort of trespass occurred. "*Terrorists rammed a boat into the side of a ship in Yemen,*" she screamed into my answering machine in 2000. "*Nineteen dead so far!*"

◆   ◆   ◆

"Were you . . ." I touch my own face, surprised by the heat on my cheeks. "Burned?"

Randy shakes his head. "Projectile injuries. Leg broken in a couple of places, a concussion." He touches his left temple. "Got a scar here. Not sure what hit me, but all sorts of shit was flying through the air."

"Man. That's crazy."

"My injuries, they weren't much. It's what I saw. The others."

I look back up at the sky, at the loneliest star or the largest planet. "Were any of them . . . were they your friends?"

"They were kids. Nineteen, twenty. I was thirty-two, this old man." He laughs, then stops laughing and shakes his head. "Those motherfuckers put a fourty-by-six-foot gash in the hull. It's a miracle more didn't die."

"The hole in the plane was twenty inches," I say.

He looks over at me in the cold moonlight. "Twenty inches? Seriously?"

"At 31,000 feet, twenty inches becomes a whole lot more pretty fast."

"I'd kill him if I could," Randy says. "The guy who put the bomb on that plane. With my own bare hands, if I had to."

I know he means it. Other people mean it in theory—they *want* to mean it—but they would never carry it through. But I know Randy would, could, kill the bomber, given the chance.

"You're shivering," he notices. "We should probably get out of the cold."

We step through the dark back to Randy's truck. He opens the door and holds out his arm to help me hoist myself into the cab. I grab him there, and he grabs me back, his whole hand circling my wrist. I'm not sure who pulls, who pushes, what makes the space between us collapse.

Randy's lips are cold and dry, but his hands are warm.

In Randy's SUV, coats come off, jeans, then underwear. He pulls out his wallet and he pulls out a condom and he pulls it on over him. I climb on his lap and rise and then fall and we gasp. I move against him fast.

Randy puts his hands on my hips. "Slow down, sugar." His drawl is strong. "I'm almost on my way."

I don't slow down. I don't want to stop, but I also want this to be over with. Randy could slow me, if he wanted to. His hands are big enough and strong enough to hold my hips still, but he lets them drop away, alongside his thighs.

Randy's jaw twists and his eyes close so hard that lines bisect his forehead. He lets the sound rise up from deep inside. And I finally feel it: everything in Randy goes weak. His limbs fall limp and, for just a few seconds, I know I can hurt him. I could kill him if I wanted to.

I don't speak when Randy drops me off. What is there to say, really? *It was nice meeting you. Try not to get shot by all that noise.* I go straight to my bedroom and open the closet door. I press myself into a dark corner. I close myself inside.

Sometime around midnight—sometime after I stop crying and shaking—I pick myself up from the closet and into bed. Even if I could sleep in there—which I can't—then what? I'd wake up with a sore neck and a pain in my back and I'd have to explain why Jack found me sleeping in the closet. It's too pathetic.

I'm in bed when Jack pulls back the comforter and slides in next to me at 8 a.m. "How were the stars?" I whisper.

"Dusty," he says.

"I know." I pull Jack's arm tighter around my ribcage. "I looked, but didn't see anything good."

Jack falls asleep and snores. Like he's gasping for air with every second of his dreams. His exhales blow air onto the back of my head. It cools my skull.

Usually, I like having Mondays off. I get to sleep in and drink coffee and do simple errands while everyone else trudges through rush hour traffic and sits in a cubicle. On the Monday morning after Thanksgiving, after I've kissed Jack goodbye and wished him a good day at work, I see my house. It's a mess. There's a basket of unwashed flannel sheets still sitting in the foyer. The Sunday paper is scattered over the living room floor. Crumbs from the tops of muffins litter the kitchen table.

I wipe crumbs off the table, I toss them in the trash. I load sheets into the washing machine. I shake each one out before layering them in the machine, so they won't spin into a twisted mess. I gather all the sections of *The Gazette* strewn about the living room. I make sure they line up and fold, and I place them in their original order: Section A, B, C, Living, and so on.

I know these simple acts won't fully erase the mess of the weekend. But I have to clean up what I can.

The doorbell rings. Mandy's on the front porch. For once, she's not wearing that hideous orange lipstick. Her bare lips are rosy, a flush that's romantic and benign.

"Do you have our muffin tin?" she asks.

"Oh. Yes. Hang on, I'll get it for you." I start to close the door, but Mandy pushes it open, follows me to the kitchen.

"Why aren't you in school?" I ask.

The tin's sitting on the kitchen counter covered by plastic wrap. Three muffins remain. "You wanna keep those?" Mandy asks. "They were good, right? I mean, I'm not bragging or anything. It's not like I invented them. I just followed the recipe."

"No," I say. "I mean, yes. They were delicious. Like pumpkin pie, but . . . muffiny."

"Jack had some, right?" Mandy eyes the tin suspiciously. "I mean, they were for Jack, too. Not just you."

"He had at least six." He'd even heated one up and topped it with vanilla ice cream. Jack will turn anything into an ice cream sundae. He'd do it to the stars, if he could.

I excavate the remaining muffins with the edge of a butter knife and transfer them to a dinner plate. "Thanks again."

Mandy looks into the empty muffin cups, like she might find something more precious than crumbs clinging to the Teflon. She looks and she looks, like she might never give up. "My dad left this morning."

I'd heard Randy's engine turn over at 5 a.m. It was cold and dark, and he let it run for ten minutes before gears shifted and the hum become fainter as it propelled him away.

"He might get deployed one more time," Mandy says. "I don't know. It's too bad there's no Navy bases here. But why would you need a Navy base in Colorado Springs, right?" She looks up. I see that her eyeliner is smudged. The smudges are at least a few hours old. "Jack and my dad," Mandy says, "They're pretty different."

I wonder if guilt operates at all like grief? If it tries to make its way out of your pores, if you can push it back down into your viscera.

I'm sure as fuck going to try.

"Jack likes cupcakes," I say. "His favorite is chocolate with coconut on top."

"Like, a brown snowball? That's gross."

"A little," I agree. Especially when she puts it that way. "I have a recipe, if you want it."

"Sure." Mandy nods her head, again mining for treasure in the recesses of the muffin tin. "Do you have any of those little paper cup thingies?"

I open the cupboard next to the stove. "And pretty much all the ingredients."

I set the ingredients on the counter, the flour and sugar, the baking soda and salt, the cocoa and vanilla and oil. I take the muffin tin from Mandy's hands, instigating an infinitesimal tug of war between us. I'm not entirely sure who pushes, who pulls. Mandy releases the pan. I take it to the sink, fill each hole with warm water and soap. We let the tin soak while I measure and Mandy stirs.

i see you in the bright night

I fold over the stack of ones and fives and slide them inside the pocket of my blond leather coat. Seven crisp and new, another seven with corners folded, and twelve crumpled and dirty. A pretty bad take, even for a weeknight. Too many guys there mainly for the six-dollar steak, black crisscross on top, sanguine inside. Women tip best—it makes them feel like feminists—and there wasn't one out there tonight. Not that I could see, anyway. Not that I looked real hard.

"Night, Sabrina," Jenna says as I come down the back stairs. She's leaning against the brick wall with that creepy boyfriend leaning against her. He's the kind of guy who goes around bragging to his buddies that his girlfriend's a stripper, and she's too dumb to realize that's not the kind of proud you want your boyfriend to be.

"You need a ride home?" the creepy boyfriend asks. He asks me this nearly every night, even on ones when Jenna's not there.

"No, I'm good."

Someone should bother to clean up this asphalt. It's nothing but a parking lot outside a bar on Colfax, but there just aren't that many pretty sights late at night. The Rocky Mountains melted away hours ago, and it's too bright to see the stars. Light pollution, they call it. We get it on both ends, a brown cloud during the day and a blinding haze at night. So even though a piece of blacktop might not seem like much, it would make a difference to have the cigarette butts

swept up and the oil stains cleaned off. You can do that with plain
kitchen cornstarch. Mama taught me that, because Mike hated when
grease leaked from the barbeque grill onto the concrete porch. You
had to clean it up right away, as soon as it dripped down, instead of
waiting until after dinner, otherwise Mike couldn't eat. And if Mike
couldn't eat, then Mama and I couldn't eat, either.

"It ain't safe for you to be walkin' home by yourself," Jenna's boyfriend
calls, but I'm already far enough away that I don't have to answer.

You'd think it would be true, that it's not safe for a woman to be
walking alone on Colfax late at night, but it's a funny thing: the later
it is, the safer it becomes. Men who hurt women aren't any different
from regular folks in that way. At two-thirty in the morning they
want to be home in bed with their wives or girlfriends, or whoever.
At two-thirty in the morning even the bums are asleep in the
doorways of closed-up businesses, and the only people I see are
kids, barely twenty-one, in black boots and studded denim jackets
and ripped black jeans. They're buzzed from drugs at some club,
trying to decide if they're going to go home and sleep it off, or keep
looking for another party.

The door to my building—four stories of red brick and black
fire escapes, the kind that suburban kids dream of escaping to—is
unlocked. It's supposed to be a secure building, but the lock has
been broken for months and no one's bothered to fix it. Maybe no
one's bothered to complain. I walk up one flight of starkly lit stairs
and there's Kort, slumped-over sleeping in front of my door. Sable
suede jacket, faded blue jeans with one ripped knee, black leather
boots. I don't know how anyone could sleep in the bare light bulb
bright, but his eyes are closed. He looks peaceful. Innocent.

Kort hasn't been innocent for a good fifteen years, not since before
we lost our virginity to each other back in Texas. It was in his bedroom
after school, even though he hadn't gone to school that day.
Sometimes it was easier to skip school than to make up excuses. We
were almost always alone at Kort's house, since his mama died when
he was nine and his dad worked until six. His dad was real kind to
me if he came home right after work, because that meant he hadn't
been drinking yet. He always offered me a Coke, and a couple of
times even asked me to stay for supper. We just had Hamburger
Helper and green beans from a can with Italian salad dressing to

flavor them up. Kort made fruit cocktail mixed with Cool Whip for dessert. I know that's not what people call good food, but I'd eat it again if someone put it in front of me.

I bend down and stretch my hand out toward Kort's suede shoulder. His arm flies out, hard and straight like a crowbar, to swat me away. His whole body convulses upright, and his blue-gray eyes go wide. They're underlined by crescent moons stained dark by red and blue make purple. "Sab," he says. "Sorry. I didn't know it was you."

"It's okay." I know there's no good way to wake people like us in the middle of the night. "How long you been here?"

"I don't know." He squeezes his blue-gray eyes shut. Not sky blue, the color of boy-next-door seducers, and not gray, like someone who doesn't give a shit. Blue-gray. "An hour, maybe."

I twist my key in the deadbolt. "Come on in."

My apartment is stuffy from being closed up all day. I push my two windows open, and pull aside the red paisley curtains I sewed out of fabric from Goodwill. Kort slides out of his jacket and tosses it across records upright in a plastic bin. Clapton. Sex Pistols. Femmes. His boots clomp against the scratched hardwood as he walks to the futon next to my east window. Both my windows face south, but I call the one on the left side my east window. The one on the right is west. In the morning, I only pull open the paisley curtain on the east window; in the afternoon, the one over the west.

"You want some tea or a beer?" I ask.

"Tea would be good."

I run water into the silver tea kettle, turning metal cold. "I haven't seen you for a while."

"Yeah, well . . ." He pulls a rubber band out of his matted blond hair, smoothes it down and back with his fingers, then pulls the length through the rubber band again. "I've been pretty busy fucking up my life."

"That's hard to believe," I say. "The last time I saw you, you were a picture of self-confidence. You were also in love." She was smart and kind, he told me. Educated at a real college—like him. Not in community colleges spattered through towns leading away from Houston. Studio Painting here, Elementary Ethics there, Poetry everywhere. She was also from a good family, the right kind of girl for someone like Kort.

"Well, being in love isn't all it's cracked up to be," he says.

"Depends on who you talk to," I say. "Some people actually like it."

"Well, some people are better at it than I am. It's been a long time since I've gotten it right." He inhales through his nose like the air is sprinkled sweet with rain and he just wants to smell it. Taste it. Absorb it all. "Maybe the only time I ever got it right was with you."

"Well, that doesn't count." Not because we were fifteen. Because he ran away. Because one night after his dad passed out, Kort stole all the money from his wallet and jumped onto a bus with his backpack and guitar. He didn't call me until a month after he got to his big sister's apartment in Berkeley. He was afraid I'd be in trouble if I knew.

The kettle whistles, although I don't know why it's called that. It's more like a shriek, when all the pressure has built up inside and the only way to let it all out is with a good scream. I pour the hot water into two coffee mugs that I stole from a diner on Broadway. Kort looks better now than when I first woke him, but not as good as when we first ran into each other two months ago. It was at the record store where I work, my day job, the one I tell people about when they ask what I do. I was crouched behind the counter with a razor in my hand, slicing through fibrous brown tape on a cardboard box. He asked my co-worker if we carried used vinyl. Even though his voice had lost the slow Texas drawl, the sound of it made me hot. Sticky. I unfolded my body and went tall—like how you stretch out one of those paper lanterns over a light bulb. Make it pretty. I said his name with an old twang, then his sunglasses fumbled out of his fingers, onto the floor.

Peppermint steam tingles in my nose. I hand Kort a hot cup. "Honey?"

"Please." He huddles in, meets the rising steam.

I pick up the amber plastic bear from the counter—Francis, that's what I named him. I never throw him out, just refill him from a vat at the hippie co-op—and sit next to Kort on the futon. Francis dangles upside down over Kort's mug, a gold stream, sticky sweet, dropping down. Kort smiles at me like how you think grateful should look, small and string-thin, but real, then looks into his mug. His smile goes away fast, like he sees something in there, something black and cold. "I was always sorry I didn't take you with me."

I shake my head. "You were just a kid."

"I shouldn't have left you there, with him." He keeps looking into his tea, but I wish he'd look at me, because there's something swirling in that liquid that makes him taste regret.

"I could've left, like you did," I say. "I didn't." Because by then it didn't really matter anymore. I'd gotten too old, too risky. Especially after Kort ran away. Before that, if I'd gotten pregnant Mike could've blamed it on Kort. "That delinquent knocked the little whore up," he would've said to Mama. But after Kort, there was no one left for blame.

His eyes rise up. "I was at the club tonight. Did you see me?"

"No." I look to the east, I look to the west, I look at plastic bins, at Clapton and Sex Pistols and Femmes. No, I didn't see you, no, don't come to work to see me, no, I swear I'm never going back there again, to those dank walls infected with stale cigarette smoke, because I swear this isn't me. No, I'm not one of those girls who does it for the power. You know the myth, that some man took your power away a long time ago, and you get it back by being on stage. Your body, their bodies—all under your control. I do it because for someone like me, there's no other way to make good money.

"I don't see faces," I say.

"I stood in the back," Kort says. "You were beautiful."

"Yeah, that's some beauty contest."

He's got one hand cupping his mug, another resting on his knee, but I want it to be resting on me, so I know he sees me here, not there, on stage in costume, then not.

"You were so sexy. So sweet." His voice drifts and fades, goes searching in the corners of the room, and I hope it never finds its way back. Just falls away thinking of me sweet. "It wasn't very crowded, you know, but there was this one guy . . . this asshole hooting and hollering. Some fucking frat boy. Teasing you with dollar bills, like you were a goddamn trained seal, or something." Kort swallows hard, and his voice goes down his throat. "I was this close to beating the crap out of him."

I shake inside and feel it peeling away, sliding across my hardwood floors, this tightly wound ribbon—it's white silk, see?— that holds the pieces in place and allows me to live this life, to be what I am, but I want to be who I am instead, who Kort thinks I am, and maybe if he could see the ribbon come undone, watch it flutter and wisp in my windows' dark night draft, he'd know how badly I want him to take me away. He could be that guy—couldn't he?—that guy in the movies who's gentle and strong and knows what's right and what's wrong and carries the girl off stage and treats her like a princess and protects her from the men who make her a whore. He could have picked me up, at the very least grabbed my hand, could have taken me with him on that bus with his backpack and his guitar, and I would have stolen money, too, from the empty coffee can that Mama kept hidden back behind the sugar in case of emergencies, in case she ever got the guts to leave. It was still there when I left, I bet it's still sitting there now.

Kort crosses his ankles in front of him, his legs tied up in a denim bow—Indian style, we used to call it, back when it was okay to call it that. I do the same and face him, the points of our knees touching, then not touching, then touching again. Kort says, "I saw my dad last week."

"Here?"

"He tracks me down about once a year, uses the baseball games he's covering as an excuse for being in town. Guess the Astros played the Rockies last week." Kort shrugs like he's trying to toss something off his shoulders. "When I see him, I just . . . I want him to know, to think, that I turned out fine." His eyes watch my red curtains sway in the breeze, paisleys dancing through the air. "My girlfriend breaking up with me . . . losing my job . . . it's hard to seem fine. So, it turned into this big melodramatic scene with lots of booze and pills and forced puking."

"That's nothing new with him, right?"

"Well . . ." He looks into his tea, laughs the nothing's-really-funny-laugh. "Pop's in AA. One year, twenty-two days, and counting. First time in his life. I was the one puking up tequila and Valium. I just wanted to steady my nerves. But I guess I went overboard."

I see Kort's nerve endings, live wires crackling, jumping about randomly, trying to find a place to land—hopefully in a pool of water to spread quickly—and it's all a lie. Trying to steady them. Numbness, that's what Kort was going for. Beating those nerves into submission through booze and drugs and sex and distance from what made you this way.

"Good," I say. "I hope he knows now what he did to you."

"But that's the thing, Sab." He's still staring at the tea that Francis made sweet and thick and gold, his eyes threatening to make it salty, too. "It got me thinking. After all these years, he's pulling his life together, and I'm more fucked up than ever. So, when's it not his fault anymore? When's it just me being weak?"

My hand reaches to his knee, to the exposed flesh peaking out from the soft, ripped threads. I slide my palm up along the cotton blue. His eyelids drop half-closed. The air was hot and sticky. It was a Texas spring day, after school. But he had skipped school that day, rather than make excuses. There were only so many times the teachers would buy that he got in a fight on his way to school. His bedroom bright, his skin white but stained purple, he fights against me to keep his T-shirt on, but I won't let him. I won't be able to hide, so neither can he. I kiss that patchwork of colors with butterflies and he almost cries, but kisses my lips instead, kisses and cups my tiny breasts, and he unbuttons my cut-off 501s and I say go slow, and he does. His hand is warm, filling the small space between my shorts and those curly hairs darker than the ones on my head, a finger exploring through creases inside creases, and I am hot. Sticky. Wet. My hand on the top button of his 501s, not cut-off, pulling over his slim hips, boy hips, bare ass, a boy's ass, and boy hard. This is what a boy, hard, feels like, not that much smaller than a man, not that much softer, but kinder. He has a condom, because he knows it's risky. He covers the purple veins, makes them shiny. Contained. Safe. When he slides inside me slow, it doesn't hurt, not like it's supposed to hurt your first time because it's not my first time, but it is, and my eyes water because I want it to hurt with him and no one else. I want it to hurt the way it's supposed to. Then Kort speaks. He tells me to look at him, to see his eyes, not blue and not gray, to stay there with him in his bedroom, bright.

Red paisleys dance in the night. I set my tepid mug on the floor next to the futon, and Kort does the same. My hand moves up his thigh, past his crotch, over his belly, soft, up his chest, hard like a man, and I push him back. My pillows catch him. I slide my curvy hips, full breasts along the cotton comforter, alongside his ribs, and settle in. My ear rests against his chest. Ba-boom. Ba-boom. Ba-boom.

"Close your eyes," I say. "You need sleep."

His arm moves across us both, and pulls me to him tight. His eyes close and mine stay open while I listen to the air shushing between his lips, to the ba-boom, ba-boom, until they are both quiet, deep, slow.

In the morning it will be bright, blue outside my windows east and west, inside my curtains red, and no more purple beneath Kort's eyes.

a note from the author

First and foremost, I want to thank Kevin Morgan Watson at Press 53 for his support. There is nothing as transcendental as when a publisher *gets* your stories. A big shout-out goes to Gigi Little for designing the beautiful cover. Several stories in this collection were previously published and I am grateful to all the editors who championed my work, most especially, David Leavitt. Thank you to The Sewanee Writers Conference for awarding me a Tennessee Williams Scholarship, and the Tin House Summer Workshop for putting up with me year after year. The extraordinary Tin House instructors not only taught me how to write, but how to be a writer. I have endless gratitude for Aimee Bender, Charlie D'Ambrosio, Tony Doerr, Jim Shepard, and especially Steve Almond, who kicked my ass on almost every story I ever wrote—to the point that I swore I'd never consult him again ("He just doesn't *get* me!"), but I kept going back, because he really, *really* gets it. Tremendous thanks to The Attic Institute, where Merridawn Duckler taught my first writing class, David Biespiel gave me my first teaching job, and my students taught me about the love of stories. Like so many writers in Portland, I am indebted to Joanna Rose and Stevan Allred of the Pinewood Table for always listening for my song. Around every critique table I've sat at over the years was a luminous solar system of smart, generous writers who gave me priceless feedback and support and friendship, way too many to list individually, so let's go with: If you were in a writing class or group with me, I seriously heart you.

The friendship (literary and otherwise) of Yuvi Zalkow, Jackie Shannon Hollis, Laura Stanfill, Gaynl Keefe, the folks at Annie Bloom's Books, and Michelle DeShong has been a constant saving grace, propelling me forward when I needed it, and giving me a soft place to land when I needed that, too. Extra love goes to Annie Lareau for letting me borrow her loss and turn it into something else. I never forgot it was her heart beating beneath the words.

My mom, Janice Prato, believed in me more than anyone on this earth, and I wish she was here to share and read and laugh and cry and hug and laugh some more with me.

More than anyone in this universe and all its possible multiverses, every single day I thank those exploding stars for sending me my best friend, my love, my partner in silliness, Michael Keefe. You are the center of it all.

Liz Prato writes in Portland, Oregon, and edits and teaches everywhere. Her work has appeared in numerous publications, including *Hayden's Ferry Review, The Rumpus, Iron Horse Literary Review, Hunger Mountain*, and *Subtropics*. She is the editor of the fiction anthology *The Night, and the Rain, and the River*. Liz spends an inordinate amount of time just watching her pets with her husband, who is a musician, writer, and bookseller. Visit her at www.lizprato.com

Cover artist GIGI LITTLE is a graphic artist, book cover designer, children's book illustrator, fiction editor, and writer. By day, she's the Lead Visual Merchandiser for Powell's Books in Portland. Her stories and essays have appeared in several journals and anthologies, including *Portland Noir, Brave on the Page, Thumbnail,* and *NAILED.* Before moving to Portland, Gigi spent fifteen years in the circus as a lighting director and professional clown. She never took a pie to the face, but she's a Rhodes Scholar in the art of losing her pants. Visit her online at gigilittle.jimdo.com.